THE
BELLTREES
INCIDENT
THE BUNKER

Elizabeth Munton

THE BELLTREES INCIDENT

Copyright

Text copyright © Elizabeth Munton, 2020

Cover design by Grzegorz Japoł,
book-cover.design

Disclaimer

This book is a book of fiction. Names, characters, places and incidents either area a creation of the author's imagination or are used fictitiously.

Resemblance to any actual events, locations, groups, or people living or dead, are coincidental and outside the intention of the author.

Acknowledgements

For my Mum, whom had little schooling helped me create stories and always listened with enthusiasm.

For Kathy, Margaret, Melinda, Rebecca, Graham and retired NSW Police Officers John and Geoff thank you all for helping me during this journey.

CHAPTER

1

It was early afternoon when the fire alarm sounded. The nonchalant behaviour of personnel soon dissipated as smoke started filling the underground bunker.

Dr Phillip Anderson, the lead scientist, yelled out, "This is not a drill; we are working in a secret bunker! Nobody knows we are here!"

Then the panic started to rise in his voice. "Hell, the master pass isn't working! I can't open any of the room doors!" He waved frantically at the others in the room. "Someone, go and open the manhole and call the fire brigade. Get out, now!"

Scientists, assistants and subjects started running up the stairs.

While the others fled from the bunker, Dr Anderson was overcome by smoke. He fell unconscious to the floor.

When the bunker lost power, the automatic doors started opening.

Ella Murphy, communications researcher, could be seen standing outside on the phone, raising the alarm, calling 000.

When the local police and fire brigade arrived at the WW II bunker outside Belltrees, sirens blaring, above ground, all that remained was shattered glass and debris.

Sergeant Parker, the first police officer on the scene, announced to all emergency services personnel present: "This appears to be a recovery mission and not a rescue. Reports are that this was a research facility. Stay focused as you walk around the site, take photos as you collect evidence," he ordered.

An officer with his arm raised called out to his superior, "Sergeant, you need to see this!"

Reaching the officer, the sergeant stopped short in disbelief. "What is that? Tag it but do not move the body. I'm going to call in reinforcements."

Parker knew he now had to contact Mid North Coast District Police Commander, Roger Smith. "Darn it," he said to himself, as his call went to voice mail.

"Area Commander Smith, this is Sergeant Parker from Belltrees Police. I am phoning you regarding the Belltrees incident. My men found something odd. I am sending you a photo. Please phone me back on this number."

It was not long before Parker's mobile rang, caller ID alerting him that it was Area Commander Smith.

"Thanks for phoning me back, sir."

"Saw your photo. Bring me up to speed. What else have you uncovered at the location?" Commander Smith asked.

"Total of four bodies found. First body looks human, other three bodies look more like robots! Reports of one, possibly two escapees running through the bush. One more thing, sir, I counted five cars in the carpark. Once they climbed out of the manhole, where did the survivors go?"

"Transport the bodies to Port Macquarie Base Hospital Forensic Medicine Division. Parker, it is imperative that all personnel from the bunker that you have identified do not speak with anyone, not even family, until after a debriefing. Is that understood, Parker?"

"Yes, sir, understood."

Texting his friend and colleague, Commander Ronald Murphy, the commander sent a short text. "Belltrees stuff-up, emailing you now."

Opening his emails, Commander Murphy read the subject line and knew what he had to do.

Replying, he typed, "Thanks, Roger. I'll take it from here. Think we need help with this one!"

CHAPTER

2

In a panic, Ella began driving down a lonely road after fleeing flames that had engulfed the old WW II bunker. Music on the radio that had been keeping her company suddenly turned to static. It was early afternoon, but the canopy of trees allowed little sunshine through. A chill ran down her spine. She felt like she was being watched.

A flash of light suddenly lit up the road ahead. What looked like a large silver robotic machine with red glowing eyes started running towards the car. Panicking, she swerved to the side as it ran past the car and disappeared into the shadows.

"What was that?"

At the exact same time, she caught a glimpse of a man and a teenager running parallel to the road. Coming to a stop, she rolled down her window slightly as she unlocked the doors and called out, "Bloody hell, are you running from that thing? Quick, hop in!"

"Thanks, it was chasing us," the boy said breathlessly.

"What are you doing out here?"

"Bushwalking. We came across what looked like an underground bunker. We forced open the manhole lid, but before we could get inside, we heard a rumbling sound, then this thing leapt out. We took off and it began chasing us. It looked like a robot on fire!" the father continued.

Up ahead, a red-eyed metallic figure suddenly turned into a ball of fire and started running towards the car.

"Like that?" Ella asked nervously.

The boy clung tightly to his father.

"Hang on!" Ella yelled, steering the car to the right and speeding away.

"I'm Tom, and this is my son Harrison," Tom announced from the back seat.

"I'm Ella."

Thirty minutes or so had passed when the radio announcer came across loud and clear.

"We interrupt this broadcast with breaking news. Police are urging everyone residing near the tiny township of Belltrees to stay inside and keep the doors locked. Reports are coming in of people being chased by a machine-like creature!"

Approaching the town centre, Ella asked, "Where would you like me to drop you off?"

"The town hall will be ok, thanks. I'll get the car tomorrow," replied Tom.

Before dropping the pair off in town, Ella wanted to share what had happened at the bunker site. But fortunately, she remembered the instructions not to tell anyone about what had happened.

"Shit, the debriefing!"

CHAPTER

3

"Belltrees, a tiny town near Barrington Tops is on the map in Australia and abroad since the story broke about the 'Mystery Machine.'

"Good morning, listeners. I'm Michael Browne, coming to you live from ABC North Coast Radio 771. Welcome to the programme. I have a busy show this morning. NSW went from the extremes of tragic bushfires to widespread flooding but much of our state is still in drought. Across the globe, tornados lashed parts of the USA.

"But first I want to start off with what has been dubbed 'The Mystery Machine.'

"As I was preparing to go on air this morning, a man, who prefers to remain anonymous, walked into the station and asked to speak with me off air.

"He was a former contract cleaner at the bunker. Apparently, he asked too many questions. The day of the fire was his last day on the job. He saw a man and boy bushwalking near the WW II bunker but didn't think too much about it.

"He also told me only a handful of personnel, including scientists, worked in the bunker. His access was limited, but one day through an open door, he saw what looked like a robot sitting on a chair. Excitedly, he told me it looked straight at him! Its eyes were almost human. And another thing, it had silver skin!

"Today at the makeshift press conference set up in the Scone RSL Club, I and other journalists watched the big screen as the Minister for Defence, Melanie Grant, approached the podium.

"The minister's speech was brief. 'In the interests of national security, there will be no statement today in relation to the incident near the town of Belltrees. Thank you and have a good afternoon.'

"For those of you who may have missed the 'incident,' let's have a recap of the events.

"Bunker personnel, including communications researcher Ella Murphy, fled the bunker as it was engulfed in flames.

"A father and son bushwalking in the area discovered a manhole lid, which they forced open – an error of judgement on their part, because something leapt out and began chasing them through the bush towards the road.

"So, is the federal government protecting the citizens of Australia from a possible national security threat?

"Was that a possible threat in the bunker? Were the scientists conducting experiments on robots?

"My telephone number is 131771. The lines are now open, give me a call."

CHAPTER

4

Children's laughter and church bells ringing in the distance from a nearby church reminded Barney why he was hiding in the bushes after fleeing the bunker fire.

Across the stream, he could see two girls sitting on a picnic blanket with their parents.

"Mummy, can Anna and I go play?" asked Grace.

"Yes, ok, but come back when I call you," said Sasha.

The girls looked at the stream, then, giggling, looked at each other. They had seen a little man waving at them, close to the water.

"Hello!" Grace said.

"What's your name?" Anna asked.

"My name is Barney," he replied.

"Barney, why are you so little?" Anna asked.

Running closer to Barney, the girls embraced each other, laughing.

Anna called out, "Come and play with us, Barney!"

The girls knelt down next to each other, excited to make a new friend.

Grace reached into her pocket and pulled out a bag of lollies. "Here, Barney, these are for you," she said.

Barney, with tears in his eyes, replied, "Thank you!"

A young boy, also playing near the stream, looked over at Grace and asked, "Who's that?" pointing to Barney.

"He is our friend Barney," she said, as she turned her back on the boy.

"Barney, we have toys under our house, want to come and play?" Anna asked. "Come on let's go," she said.

Then she let out a cry. "Where are you going? It's this way!"

Being short, Barney knew he would blend in to look like a friend of the girls.

He'd been observing the twins for a few days, watching and waiting. Today was the day he could hopefully find a hiding place, under the girls' house.

The anger he felt was intense. He didn't want to be like this. A shooting pain ran along his arms as the nerve endings received shock-like sensations. Taking a deep breath, he sighed.

The sharp triangular shadows of the church opposite the stream had penetrated deep over the pathway. A wintry wind stirred the leaves. Confused, Barney looked up to the sky, as they finally reached the house and crawled under the floor cavity.

CHAPTER

5

Opening his emails, Commander Ronald Murphy read his latest email as he phoned Central Metropolitan Commander Phillip Morgan.

"Phillip, there is a situation at Belltrees and we need your help. Please send your two best detectives to join the North Coast Task Force.

"The Minister for Defence and my contact at Pine Gap have arranged for one of their intelligence operatives to attend," he continued.

"Phillip, your detectives will be briefed upon arrival and must use discretion when in the field. This is never to be leaked."

"Yes, sir, I'll organise it straight away. Thank you, sir," Commander Morgan responded.

Senior Detective Morgan stood in his office doorway looking for Detective Walker. Catching his eye, Morgan beckoned him to his office.

"With Adams on extended leave, I am pairing you with Detective Spencer. He will be here shortly – actually, here he is now.

"Peter Walker, meet Joe Spencer your new partner. Come in, Detectives, and close the door behind you," he cautioned.

Handing each Detective a folder, Commander Morgan said, "A taskforce team has been assigned to the Belltrees Research Centre to investigate the fire and reported escapees from the bunker where they were being held. I'm sending you two to assist in the investigation.

"Familiarise yourselves with the file. The taskforce team operations manager will meet you both at the site tomorrow morning. Good luck."

Closing his eyes for a brief moment, Spencer asked his fellow detective, "Weren't you one of the detectives on that Sutton Forest manhunt case a few years back?"

Nodding, Walker ushered Spencer to his desk. Sitting down, they both opened the file and began reading.

"Hell!" Spencer exclaimed, stopping reading for a moment and eyeballing Walker.

CHAPTER

6

Darkness was beginning to settle on the tree canopy like a shroud. Earlier in the day, a dusting of snow had covered the mountains.

Hiding under the house, Barney felt safe, his new young friends unaware of who he really was.

Barney understood each season thoroughly, like the passing of one tint or shade of colour to another. He knew the minute and hour. He had been this way for so long, he didn't know the year, nor did he care. They had stripped the world from his life.

Leaving a footprint would be too risky. He meticulously negotiated his way further under the house.

Back at the park, Sasha called out, "Come on girls, time to go!"

With urgency in her voice, she asked her husband, "Can you see the girls, Graham?"

"I'll go get them, honey," he replied.

It would be dusk in a few minutes. A coating of frost would soon cover the leaves on the trees with icicles, forming diamond shapes twinkling with the last glimmers of light.

Leaving Sasha at the car, Graham made his way to the edge of the park where he had last seen the girls playing near the steam.

"Anna, Grace! Time to go!" he called.

A gentle pulling on his trouser leg got his attention.

"They went that way with a little man dressed in a costume," said the young boy, as he pointed towards the edge of the park.

"What is your name, son?" asked Graham.

"Shaun," said the boy.

Crawling under a bush and onto a pathway, Graham called out, "Anna, Grace! It's Daddy! Where are you?" He cleared branches to give himself a clear path.

Looking down, he found a hairband. *Dear God, where are you both!*

"Sasha, they're gone! A boy told me a little man dressed in a costume was with them as they left the park."

Rummaging through the car console, Graham found his mobile phone.

"I'm calling the police," he said. He quickly dialled 000.

"Fire, ambulance or police?" a female voice asked.

"Police!"

"Police," the radio operator announced.

"Hello! My name is Graham Fowler. My daughters are missing!"

"Where are you, sir?" the constable asked.

"What! At the north end of the park near Belltrees. My daughters were playing near the steam. A boy told me that they left with a little man dressed in some sort of costume."

"Police officers are on their way to your location now, sir," the constable said.

CHAPTER

7

Arriving at Port Macquarie Taskforce Headquarters, Detectives Walker and Spencer joined the crowd of police and government officials for a Belltrees incident update.

"Good morning, everyone. My name is Commander Roger Smith. Thank you all for assisting. Please work in pairs. My assistant is currently issuing each pair a walkie talkie, emergency beacon, and a brief identifying all personnel that worked in the bunker, and the escapees who are still on the loose in the national park. If you apprehend an escapee, assess the situation and only draw your taser or discharge your firearm after you have exhausted all other options."

The commander scanned the group in front of him, and finished off with, "Thank you all again and stay safe!"

Before leaving the meeting, Spencer tapped Walker on the shoulder and said quietly, "Guys in the suits are ASIO. Wonder why they are here?"

"How do you know they are ASIO?" Walker asked.

"Before I joined the police force, I did a security agency stint at Pine Gap. Second to last suit on the right, he was involved in an investigation at Pine Gap. Saw him there on a number of occasions. I'm curious," he added, and asked, "Do you mind if I have a quick catch-up and probe him a bit before we head off?"

"Only if I can tag along," Walker replied.

Approaching the exit door, Spencer asked the man in front of him, "Special Agent Brian Allan, you allowed out of Pine Gap these days?"

Shaking his hand, Special Agent Allan exclaimed, "Spencer or should I say, Detective Spencer, I didn't know you were on the investigation."

"Yes, drove up from Sydney yesterday. This is my partner, Peter Walker."

"I haven't been fully briefed, but it seems to be some secret robot bunker experiment facility gone wrong at Belltrees," the Special Agent said.

In the background, Area Commander Roger Smith called out, "Special Agent Allan, are you coming?"

Giving Spencer a slap on the upper arm, Allan said, "Let's catch up before you head back to Sydney, Spencer. Nice to meet you, Walker," he added.

Walking away, Spencer muttered, "Their presence means this is a big operation, possibly gone wrong. Let's take a look at the bunker site."

CHAPTER

8

"Good morning, listeners. I'm Michael Browne, coming to you live from ABC North Coast Radio 771. Welcome to the programme. I have another busy show for you this morning.

"News headlines:

10-year-old sisters, Anna and Grace Fowler reported missing at the Belltrees park.

"Cyclone Blake, currently located north of Broome, first cyclone identified in Australia for this season.

"Shark attack off the Queensland coast.

"First, an update on the Belltrees incident. I invited Melanie Grant, Minister for Defence to the show, but unfortunately declined, due to ministerial duties.

"Communications researcher Ella Murphy, no relation to Area Commander Murphy, has gone into hiding. Did the police find the man and boy who were bushwalking near the bunker? Four bodies found at the bunker have been taken to Port Macquarie Base Hospital, Forensic Medicine Division. Two or more escapees are still on the run.

"Police are still at the site of the incident. More than 20 taskforce personnel have arrived and will start searching the national park.

"Breaking news! ASIO agents have been spotted at the taskforce meeting.

"Our news reporter Neville King is waiting on the line and has an update on the taskforce meeting.

"Neville, you have a taskforce update?"

"Good morning, Michael. Yes, I do. A large presence of government officials, police and also ASIO have just exited the building, and Area Commander Roger Smith just held a press conference. Reporters were welcomed and told they could ask one question. My question follows."

"Area Commander, Neville King, North Coast Radio. Belltrees bunker incident: Why are ASIO agents at Belltrees? Is ASIO working with NSW Police Department in retrieving/collecting data on the bunker and relocating the participants in custody to a safe location for interrogation?"

"That's two questions, Neville. NSW Police and ASIO are working together to ensure there is no threat to the local residents, and the greater surrounding communities. Thank you. That will be all for now."

"Michael, he didn't really give much away before he left with the ASIO agents. We will have to see how this evolves."

"Thank you, Neville.

"Well listeners, what are your thoughts about ASIO being involved? My number is 131771, give me a call."

CHAPTER

9

The incident at Belltrees had caught the attention of the country and the world. Standing at the kitchen bench, Tom Walters decided they should report what they had encountered.

"Harrison, we are going to the police to make a statement about the thing on fire that chased us through the bushes" he said. "Get ready, we will leave soon."

Harrison did not argue. "Ok, Dad."

Tom and Harrison stood at the Belltrees Police Station reception desk. They were soon greeted by Sergeant Parker.

"Tom, Harrison, what brings you here?"

"We are here to make a statement. Harrison and I opened the manhole at the bunker. We are the father and son chased by the robot two days ago. When we heard on the news that people had died, I knew we had to make a statement."

"Take a seat, gentlemen; I'll get the detectives who are working on the case."

Walking out the back, Parker called out: "Detectives Walker and Spencer, Tom Walters and his son Harrison are at the front counter. They were the father and son chased by the robot after the Belltrees fire started."

Detective Walker came to the counter with recorder, pen and paper in hand. He said, "I'm Detective Walker. Please come through."

As they entered the interview room, Detective Spencer said, "Please take a seat."

Showing Tom Walters the recorder, Walker said, "Standard procedure to tape interviews."

"Sure," replied Tom.

"For the purpose of the recording, time is 9:30am. Present are Tom Walters, his son Harrison Walters, Detectives Spencer and Walker," Walker stated. "In your own words, Tom and Harrison, tell us what happened the day of the fire."

"Harrison and I were bushwalking. We had walked past the bunker dozens of times, but we had never noticed what looked like a manhole lid before," Tom said.

Harrison interjected. "I told Dad we should open the manhole lid and have a look."

"What happened when you opened the lid, Harrison?" Walker asked.

"Something jumped out. We didn't know what it was at first. We saw red bubbling, like when you cook food in a saucepan. There was no sound, just bubbling. It was then we realised it looked like a robot. Its face looked like a robot's face."

"What happened then, Tom?" Spencer asked.

"It ran past us, nearly knocking us down, and took off. It ran fast and disappeared into the bushes."

"Did you close the manhole lid, Tom?" Spencer asked.

"No," Tom said. "We were shaken up. We didn't think about anything other than getting out of there."

"Suddenly, this thing came running at us," Harrison continued. "We hid under a huge tree branch. It stopped and started tilting its head from side to side. Looked like it was waiting for a command, you know, like instructions."

"After a while, we heard the sound of a car's engine. The robot must have heard it too because it disappeared," Tom said. "Thinking it was safe, we started running parallel to the road, hoping the driver would see us. The woman driving saw us, stopped and called out to us to hop in her car, and we drove away. We don't even know her name. She dropped us off in town," Tom finished.

"Thank you both for coming in. Interview ended 11:30am," Spencer said. He stood up to escort Tom and Harrison from the room.

Returning to Walker, he said, "We have to find the driver."

CHAPTER

10

Heading back to the park, the girls decided Barney was their secret.

"We can't tell anyone about Barney, Anna, not even Mummy and Daddy," Grace said.

"Yes, it's our secret!" Anna replied.

Anna became distracted by small coloured round stones by the stream. "Look, Grace, we can collect these for Barney. He can play marbles with these."

Approaching the park, Constable Stanley asked her partner Constable Black for a description of the missing sisters.

"Twins Grace and Anna, aged 10, Caucasian, blonde hair, wearing matching blue tops and beige pants," responded Constable Black.

"I think we have located the missing girls," Stanley said.

Approaching the stream, she said, "Hello, my name is Constable Stanley. Which one of you is Grace?"

"Me, and this is my sister Anna."

Stepping away from the girls, Constable Stanley phoned Graham Fowler on his mobile.

"Mr Fowler, Constable Stanley here. We have located your daughters near the stream at the park. Looks like they have been collecting coloured stones," she said. "We will walk them up to you now."

Sasha and Graham could not hide their joy seeing their daughters, calling out their names as they approached.

"Anna! Grace! Where have been you been?" Sasha asked.

Holding hands, the girls said, "We have been collecting coloured stones."

"Look, Mummy!" Grace said.

Graham thanked the constables and turned to the girls. "Come on, girls. Let's go home."

Grace looked at Anna. "Remember our secret!" she whispered.

CHAPTER

11

Daisy knew the routine. Front door opens, car beeps, hatch opens, and Daisy jumps in the back and settles herself on her seat, ready to go.

Sitting at the front door with the leash in her mouth, ready to go on her daily walk, she looked eagerly at her master.

"Ok, Daisy! I'm coming!"

Grabbing her keys, Helen watched Daisy as her tail started wagging out of instinct, the keys being the stimulus. *If you could talk, you would be saying, "At last, let's go!"* Helen thought.

When the car arrived at the park, Daisy waited for Helen to open the hatch and put on her leash.

"Lots of smells today, Daisy?" Helen commented, as her dog began stopping at every tree to mark her territory as a show of dominance.

Suddenly, Daisy pulled on the leash, stopped, and started growling.

"What's up, girl?"

Bending down to pat her dog, Helen pulled the leash and took a step back. *Shit! What is that?*

Under a tree she could see what looked like a man with severe burns and silver skin.

"Please don't be frightened," said the man. "My name is Alex, Dr Alex Marinov. I have been working in the bunker at Belltrees. There was a fire and we all ran for our lives."

"Yes, it was on the news. You don't look so good. You know your skin is a silvery burnt colour, don't you?" Helen asked.

Smiling, the doctor said, "Yes, I was experimenting on myself."

"I'll call for an ambulance. You need to get to hospital!" Helen urged.

"No, please don't do that. Do you have a mobile phone with you?"

"Yes, do you need to phone someone?"

"No, but thank you for asking. I am dying but I need to make a recording and I would like you to deliver it to the media for me. We, the scientists, were experimenting on people. We were wrong. I can't trust the police or the government.

"I have a contact at ABC North Coast Radio, Michael Browne. If you allow me to make a recording, I need you to deliver it in person to Michael," he said.

Setting the phone up for the doctor, Helen sat down with Daisy as he started the recording.

Hello, Michael. It's Alex Marinov. I have been working with other scientists in the bunker near Belltrees. We have been experimenting on humans, transforming them to appear as humanoid cyborgs. As you know, there was a fire at the bunker site this week. I am not sure how many of my colleagues and subjects survived the fire.

I secretly recorded a meeting between myself, Special Agent Allan and another man who identified himself only as a government representative. He said the government was getting nervous. Apparently, it was agreed that there would be 10 candidates transformed and Allan hadn't held his side of the agreement.

We have 30 days to give him something to show evidence that the trial has been successful.

Agent Allan said someone called Henry had transformed several other candidates but only one was successful. The remaining candidates are being held captive in all bunkers.

This man was serious. We can't release these people back into the broader community.

He is waiting for the "slightly backward child to be transformed, to have a brilliant mind, and become a lethal weapon!"

I would not allow this young girl to be experimented on. I tried to keep her in a small room to be safe. I am not sure if she escaped the fire. Can you please look into this? Call it a favour!

Agent Allan said he would create a diversion, a fire in the bunker. Allan was going to escort all survivors out of the bunker, including the girl, into hiding.

A secret organisation and the government body within the Australian Government have been controlling not only this bunker but six other bunkers, one in each state. My credentials do not allow me to confirm their locations, but they do exist.

Michael, I have experimented on myself. I have red glowing eyes and silver skin. On the night of the fire, I saw Ella Murphy driving away. Ella knew nothing about why she was employed at the bunker and had no part in the experimentation. When I escaped the fire, I did chase a father and son. I meant them no harm.

Some of the subjects have had part of their brain matter partially removed. These subjects have microchips in their brain cavity and are being controlled by handlers. If approached, they will look like a confused dog waiting for instructions by tilting their head from side to side. Their handler will be watching their movements.

Their hearing has been enhanced with cochlear implants and each has been fitted with either blue or green contact lenses. Some even have GPS trackers fitted.

I am dying, Michael, and do not have much time left.

I am sorry to burden you with this, my friend, but this needs to be exposed.

Thank you,

Alex Marinov

Before leaving, Helen said, "Let me drive you to the hospital. Is there anyone I can call for you?"

"I need one more favour from you, Helen. In my pocket there is a key to a safety deposit box. It contains my life's work, including my journal. I need you to keep this safe. Don't tell anyone that you have this key, not even Michael right now. You will know when the time is right to tell Michael. Can you do this for me?"

Nodding, Helen said, "Yes, of course. What are you going to do? You can't hide under this tree forever."

"No, but after I am gone, please phone the authorities and tell them you found me, or, should I say, your dog found me."

Before Helen could utter another word, the doctor pulled a syringe from his burnt clothing and injected himself.

Helen had been shocked by what Dr Marinov had said in the recording and was even more shocked when he ended his life in front of her.

It took her a few minutes to compose herself enough to dial 000. She reported that she had found a dead man in the park.

CHAPTER

12

Since escaping from the bunker inferno, Gavin had been running. The silence was surreal. As he passed deserted campsites, childhood memories were tormenting him: family weekends away, cooking on a campfire and jovial voices singing in the rain.

He recalled being the frightened boy always hiding behind the cabin, and vividly remembered his father returning from the trees with blood dripping from an axe. His father called it "cleansing."

Gavin never liked going camping with his father. He was good at keeping secrets and never told his mother what he saw on those weekends.

Other than ground-dwelling insects and beetles running in confused circles ahead of him, nothing stirred until the encounter with a woman walking in the area. The human part of him felt remorseful for pushing the woman to the ground as he ran through the bush.

"Get to the cabin," a voice whispered to him. His handler had told him over and over: if you ever have to leave, find the cabin and hide.

Reaching the cabin, his body stiffened as he opened the door and walked inside. Standing inside, his handler said, "You made it. Are you injured?"

"No," Gavin replied.

Understanding Gavin and triggers that changed his behaviour, the handler passed him a bloody axe, blood still dripping, following a recent animal kill.

"You must remain behind the curtain and be very quiet. Soon you will play a game of hide and seek," he continued.

Gavin suddenly started convulsing, involuntary movements causing his body to fall the floor. The handler dragged his body behind the curtain.

Removing a battery pack from his bag, he attached electrodes to parts of Gavin's body and pressed a reset button. During the charge, he updated data from the chip embedded in Gavin's brain, sending them to HQ to analyse.

Before leaving the cabin, he set a timer on the chip to wake Gavin.

CHAPTER
13

Matt had been hiking in the national park near Barrington Tops all year, but this time was different. This time it was unknown territory. Struggling, walking through the roots and brambles, he stumbled, tearing his jeans and collecting thorns as he skidded on the muddy ground.

The sun glowed through the dark branches of tall trees. "Shit!" he cried, as he began to remove thorns from his legs.

A movement by his feet. The muscles in his back tensed. His heart was racing.

Mud covered an outstretched hand trying to reach up to him. Quietly, a frightened female voice asked, "Is he still here?"

Kneeling in the mud as he surveyed his surroundings, Matt asked, "Who?"

Eyeballing him as she grabbed his shirt, the young woman repeated her question. "Is he still here?"

"No-one is here, only me. Are you injured? Can you stand?" he asked.

Feeling woozy, she managed to stand whilst leaning on him.

Matt passed his water bottle to her and said, "I'm Matt Peters. What are you doing out here?"

"Kerry, I'm a volunteer with the Port Macquarie Koala Hospital. Following the recent bushfires, disorientated koalas have left their habitat, and some have been reported to be in this area. Someone or something was running through the bushes and pushed me to the ground.

"It stopped and turned to face me. Even though the face looked human, it was like someone was remotely controlling it. Then it ran off."

"The light will be fading soon. I passed a cabin about half a kilometre from here. Can you walk?" Matt asked.

Kerry nodded and they began the walk to the cabin.

After what seemed an eternity, they arrived. Grabbing the edges of Kerry's jumper, Matt opened the door and helped her inside.

The cabin was sparse.

"Ah, no chairs. Let me help you to sit on the floor. I'll take a look around."

A makeshift curtain gave the appearance of two rooms in the cabin. Pulling the curtain back, Matt was surprised to see an unusual looking man. The man rushed towards him.

Kerry called out, "That's him! He's the one who pushed me down!"

Matt yelled out, "Stop!"

Brandishing the axe and speaking gibberish, the strange man lunged towards Matt, striking him on the side of his head with the axe handle. Matt fell to the floor.

Turning to face Kerry, he stared at her as if waiting for instructions.

Digging her heels into the floor her voice echoed her desperation as she said, "please don't hurt me!"

Tilting his head slightly, he dropped the axe and began fumbling in his pockets as he removed a piece of rope and a small rag. He then proceeded to tie her hands together before forcing the rag in her mouth which made her gag.

As tears began rolling down Kerry's face, he looked straight at her and for a brief moment she thought there was sense of sadness in his eyes. He then turned around and pulled the curtain across the room as if to hide Matt behind the curtain.

CHAPTER

14

Police presence was minimal at the carpark adjacent to the bunker. Showing their visitors' authority ID, the detectives were allowed to walk freely around the incident location.

Not realising that Walker had wandered off to the right, Spencer heard him call out, "Over here, Spencer. Looks like a manhole lid. Want to take a look?"

"Hell, yeah!"

As they opened the manhole lid, smoke hit them in the face but quickly disappeared in the slight breeze. With their torches on, they cautiously climbed down a short stairway that led to an open area underground.

"Well, this is a surprise. I count 12 single rooms, each separated only by glass walls. Looks like this is where they housed the participants," Walker said. "12 single rooms. Four bodies, two or possibly three escapees. What happened to the remainder? Where are the scientists?"

Click, click echoed in the underground bunker as they both took photos as evidence.

"Looks like someone has been here and removed the electrical equipment. See, loose wire housing but no sign of equipment. This was a rushed job," Walker said, as he picked up and bagged what looked like a discarded implant.

"Last night I was reading up on transhumanism experiments, cyborgs and electronic tattoos, implants under the skin. I thought the bionic man was years away," Spencer said. "We should start walking the track, but I would like to revisit this for a closer look."

Turning around, Walker removed his glock and pointed it towards a slightly ajar door. "Police, come out!" he ordered.

To their surprise, a girl of about 16 years stepped out of a room.

"She looks confused mate, trying to pinpoint the location of sounds. Can she see us? Is she waiting for instructions?" Walker wondered.

"Lower your weapon. I don't think she can see us," Spencer said.

The girl seemed at ease as the detectives walked her up the stairway and out of the manhole.

"Officers!" Walker called out. "Can one of you escort this girl to the hospital, please?"

The girl looked in Walker's direction and hesitated for a second before saying in a soft voice, "Thank you!"

CHAPTER

15

The detectives had been following the track for 20 minutes when they stumbled across what looked like an abandoned cabin.

The sound of twigs snapping on the ground made them aware that they were not alone.

"I'll go around the back, see if there is another door," Walker whispered to his partner.

"Looks deserted," Spencer said, as he stepped up onto the porch.

Returning to his partner, Walker reported, "No entrance from the back."

Spencer heard a knocking noise. "Seems to be coming from inside."

Releasing his glock, Spencer slowly opened the door. Inside he saw a woman bound by a rope with a mouth gag. Whispering he asked, "someone else here?"

Terror appeared in the woman's eyes. Nodding, she forced her heels against the floor, trying to slide backwards.

Slowly opening the curtain, Spencer called out to his partner, "Definitely been a struggle, man unconscious here."

Securing his glock in its holster, Walker approached the woman and released her from the ropes and gag.

"I'm Detective Walker. What is your name?" he asked.

"Kerry Taylor. Is Matt alive?" she asked.

"Yes. He has a head wound and is unconscious. My partner will raise the alarm and get an ambulance here."

Suddenly, a man appeared in the doorway wielding an axe. He lunged towards Detective Walker.

Protecting Walker and Kerry, Spencer pointed his taser towards the man and commanded, "Put the axe down!"

The man with the axe tilted his head to the side as if he was waiting instructions. Then, uttering gibberish, he lunged towards Spencer. This time the detective didn't hesitate. He pulled the trigger. The taser wires with probes on the ends pointed towards the attacker's legs. They immobilised the man, allowing Walker to securely restrain him with handcuffs.

Looking back at Kerry, Walker could see she was trembling. "You're safe," he reassured her.

Releasing the police radio from its buckle, Walker spoke into it. "This is Detective Walker, beacon activated. Two injured civilians requiring ambulance. Bunker escapee in custody requiring transportation to the police station."

CHAPTER

16

Dragging their backpacks behind them, Anna and Grace tried to sneak past their mother and head out the back door.

"Stop right there, young ladies! Where do you think you're going?" Sasha asked.

"Going to play, Mummy," replied Anna.

"With your backpacks? What have you got to say for yourselves, girls?"

"We are going to play with Barney."

"Who's Barney? Sasha asked.

"He is our friend and he is hiding under the house," Grace said.

"Grace, be quiet. It's our secret," Anna said sternly.

Remembering what it was like being young and having make believe friends, Sasha smiled and said, "Ok, off you go and play, but come in when I call."

Crawling under the house, the girls called out, "Where are you, Barney?"

"We brought you some biscuits! Come and play," Anna said.

"I'm hiding," Barney whispered. "Bet you can't find me."

Crawling around under the house, the girls laughed as they played hide and seek with Barney.

But Anna became confused and started crying, upset that she couldn't find him.

"Don't cry, Anna," Barney said, poking his head around the corner.

Hearing crying, Sasha thought one of the girls may have hurt herself. She grabbed her mobile and rushed outside. Crawling under the house, she gasped as she saw the girls were not alone.

"Anna, Grace, come to me now!" Sasha commanded.

"This is Barney," Grace said.

"Now, girls!" Sasha admonished.

Sasha retrieved phone from her pocket and called 000. Before the operator could utter a word, she said, "My name is Sasha Fowler. I live at 29 Rose Street, Belltrees. One of the escapees from the bunker is under my house with my children. Please come now!"

With sirens blazing, the police arrived at the address within minutes. Approaching the house, one of the officers heard, "Under here!"

Pulling the girls close to her, Sasha made way for the officers to reach Barney. They dragged him out.

The girls freed themselves from their mother and ran to Barney.

"Don't hurt him!" Anna cried out. "He is our friend!"

Barney did not resist as the police officer placed handcuffs on his wrists.

As the officer led him towards the police car, Barney turned around to look at the girls, knowing this would be the last time he would see them.

Grace cried out, "Barney, we're sorry!"

CHAPTER

17

Walker and Spencer both received a text message from Commander Roger Smith at the same time. The text read, "We have found Ella Murphy, the bunker communications research worker. This is her location. Tread carefully, we don't know what her role was in all of this. We don't want her disappearing again."

"Before I transferred to Redfern Police Station, I had the opportunity to interview an eyewitness to an incredibly horrific event. I did a little digging after dinner last night and discovered that Ella took this job as a way of a new beginning following a failed relationship and the death of her most precious possession, her dog Wally. Do you mind if I take the lead with this one" Spencer asked?

"Go right ahead," Walker replied.

Arriving at the address, Spencer knocked at the door, knowing that Ella might take longer than usual to open it.

He showed his police badge to her. "I'm Detective Spencer and this is my partner, Detective Walker. We would like to speak with you about the bunker fire. Would it be ok if we came inside?"

"Yes, come in," Ella said.

As she sat down, her skirt hem rested on her upper thighs. Spencer noticed an unusual tattoo on Ella's right outer thigh.

"That's an unusual tattoo," he remarked.

"Yes, maths student teacher high school prank. I lost a bet and so I had to get a scarecrow tattoo. I chose my thigh area, thought it wouldn't hurt that much."

"Tell us a little about your role as communications researcher at the bunker," Spencer said.

"At first, I thought the job was updating a college communications register, archiving names for people that had graduated, registering new students and organising medicals for these new students. A few weeks ago, I saw something that made me realise my employment was a coverup. I needed a job, so I didn't say a word to anyone" Ella said.

"You worked at the bunker on weekdays, correct?"

"Yes, Monday to Friday."

"Were there other people also working with you in that office environment?" Walker asked.

"No."

Taking photos from an envelope, the detective said, "I am going to show three photos. Have you met any of these men? Take your time."

Picking up the photo of Agent Allan, Ella said, "This man came in sometimes. Not sure of his name but I remember Scott used to say he was important."

Touching the second photo, Ella said, "This is Scott Kelly. I think he may have been a security guard.

"He would always arrive with what looked like a doctor's bag, remove papers and file them in a cabinet, replace them with blank papers and head downstairs. As he left in the evenings, he would take the papers out and take them with him.

Pointing to the third photo Ella said, "I never met this man."

"I befriended the cleaner, Ernie Baker, and asked him what was underground. He told me that the bunker was a research facility. He also told me that there were mainly men, of all ages, one middle-aged female and one young girl downstairs.

"He also told me only a handful of personnel, including scientists, worked below ground in the bunker. His access was limited, but one day through an open door he had seen what looked like a robot sitting on a chair. He said that when it looked at him, its eyes were almost human, and it had silver skin!

"Doing some discreet research, I found out that the bunker was a front for some sort of testing laboratory. I knew people were underground but thought they were on a course and worked in isolation.

"One day, Scott left the cabinet unlocked, so I opened a file and read it. The file called them 'subject participants'! Some of them came from poverty, crime, greed, or guilt, and the young girl had a form of autism."

"How did that make you feel?"

"Angry. Not only had they lied to me, they were using me in their cover-up. Ernie later told me they sacked him for asking too many questions."

"On Ernie's last day, I asked him how the scientists and the 'participants' downstairs exited, as I never saw them walk past me. He told me there was a manhole.

"Also, Scott handed me a package and told me to keep it safe. Looking inside, I saw it contained the participants' files."

"What did you then do, Ella?" Walker asked.

"I took the files."

Standing up, Spencer asked, "Do you have the files here, Ella?"

Ella retrieved the files from a drawer and passed them to Detective Spencer. "Am I under arrest?"

"No, but you will need to accompany us to the station to make a full statement."

Ella looked from Detective Spencer to Detective Walker, then slowly stood up. "Ok, I'll get my coat," she said quietly.

CHAPTER

18

The next morning, Walker and Spencer were having breakfast in the hotel restaurant when Area Commander Roger Smith approached their table. They both stood and greeted him.

"Would you like to join us for breakfast, Commander?" Walker asked.

Gesturing with his hands the commander said, "Relax, guys. Sit. I've already had breakfast.

"I'll be at the incident site at 10am. Meet me there when you're done here. It's important for you to gather your own intel and have your questions ready for when the ME report is issued."

Once they were at the bunker site, Walker saw that ASIO was also present. "Spencer, Special Agent Allan is also here."

Seeing the Special Agent, Spencer said, "We meet again."

Spencer and Walker made their way towards the opened manhole entrance. They saw an ununiformed man also walking to the entrance.

"This is a crime scene. Can I help you?" Walker asked.

Stepping over the yellow crime scene tape the man asked, "Any survivors? Where did they take her?"

Moving forward, Spencer asked, "Who, sir?"

The man started to walk away. "Forget it!" he said.

"Constable, please escort this man out of the area," Spencer called to a nearby officer.

Walker retrieved a notepad from his pocket. "I took some notes yesterday when we spoke with Ella Murphy."

As the detectives stepped inside the bunker, they saw that there were bright lights mounted throughout the open area. This observation was followed by the smell of urine.

Each of them took photos as they looked around. The basement had been transformed into 12 small rooms and one larger room, which looked like an examination room. All rooms had glass walls and doors.

Checking the doors, Walker commented, "No lock. This indicates that the rooms were remotely locked and un-locked. Once the participants were locked inside, there was no way out."

Standing in room 2, Spencer said, "Check this out. Blood on the floor and also the side wall. The pattern of the blood mist looks like there may have been a struggle. I will take a sample of both areas."

He continued examining the other rooms. No other clues had been left like those in room 2.

Walker noticed that Special Agent Allan was with another man, possibly another agent. "Spencer, can you take photos of all present here today?"

"Why?"

"You have heard the saying: every picture tells a story. We should be able to tell by the photos who of these people have been here before. Ensure you get photos of the ASIO agents."

"I'm with you, will do."

"Spencer, see Agent Allan down the back on the left? He is taking photos, dusting for fingerprints. To me, there is nothing in that area, but if you had been here before, would you only dust if you thought something was missing from that spot?"

Before Spencer could answer, Walker asked, "Where is Sergeant Parker?"

"I'm here, Detective. How can I help?" Parker asked.

"When you came here on the day of the fire, did the ASIO agents also come here on that day? If so, how long after you got here did you see them arrive?"

"ASIO didn't come here until yesterday," Parker replied.

"See this here. When Spencer and I were here two days ago, a young girl came out of that room," Walker said, pointing to an open door on the left.

"There were no drag marks outside the door on that day. What did they remove from the room?" he asked.

"Anything removed from the site has to be logged. I'll check the log and let you know," Parker said.

Walker looked around once more. "I think we are done here," he said.

CHAPTER

19

Commander Roger Smith and Sergeant Parker saw that Walker and Spencer were ready to leave the bunker site when they caught up with them.

"Detectives, I hope you both took lots of photos and obtained samples of any blood spills and fingerprints," said the commander.

"Yes, we have, sir," said Walker.

"Sergeant Parker, Spencer and I will go over the files that Ella Murphy took from the bunker site," he continued.

"The Forensic Medical Examiner report is available, should be in your inboxes. Dr Raelene Attard ME will be presenting her findings of the two bodies at the task-force meeting room at 1pm. Make sure you check your emails before the meeting," he finished.

Sitting at their desks, Walker and Spencer started reading the files that they had taken from Ella Murphy, in particular, finding out how the young girl fitted into the bunker scene.

"Here is her file. Her name is Susan Tanner, 16 years old, chosen due to her being intellectually challenged. How can they justify this?" Walker asked.

"Says here that she got into a bit of trouble last year. Still doesn't justify why they chose her," he added. "If you read down further, scientist Dr Alex Marinov refused to perform testing on her, so she was locked up. That must have been the room where we found her."

"Sergeant Parker, can you organise a female police officer to be present when we speak with her at the hospital, please?" he asked.

"Constable Stanley will meet you both at the hospital at 4pm when you interview Susan Tanner," Parker replied.

CHAPTER

20

The taskforce meeting room was packed with police, government officials and ASIO agents when Walker and Spencer arrived at 1pm.

Mid North Coast Local Area Commander Roger Smith opened the meeting by thanking the members of the taskforce for joint agency efforts in this unusual crime scene, the WW II Bunker site at Belltrees.

"I would like to invite Dr Raelene Attard to the podium for her findings about the two bodies retrieved from the crime scene," he said.

"Good afternoon, everyone. As Commander Smith said, my name is Dr Raelene Attard, Forensic Medical Officer at Port Macquarie Base Hospital. May I say that I would never have envisaged that I would be examining artificially enhanced humans, who I have labelled Subjects A and B. You should have received an email with my findings."

Dr Attard's email contained the following:

Subject A: Male – Caucasian, age approximately 20 years:

1. *Brain – the skull cavity has been excavated and the brain matter partially removed. Micro-stimulation electrode acts as a conduit between electrical signals – controls robot facial features, extremities.*

   A tracking device has also been implanted under the skin of the right wrist, which suggests he may be right-handed. One would assume the subject being controlled by an outside source, a handler with a joystick or like control.

2. *Eyes – blue, contact lenses.*

3. *Cochlear implants.*

4. *Extremities – subject has a sixth digit on each hand and foot, these are usually removed at birth.*

Summary:

Micro-stimulation electrode acts as a conduit between electrical signals controlling robot extremities. Cochlear implants.

Subject B: Male – Caucasian, age approximately 25 years:

1. *Brain – the skull cavity has been excavated and the brain matter partially removed. Micro-stimulation electrode acts as a conduit between electrical signals – controls robot facial features, extremities.*

A tracking device has also been implanted under the skin of the left wrist, which suggests he may be left-handed. One would assume the subject being controlled by an outside source, a handler with a joystick or like control.

2. *Eyes — green, contact lenses.*

3. *Cochlear implants.*

4. *Extremities — subject has five digits on each hand and foot.*

Summary:

Micro-stimulation electrode acts as a conduit between electrical signals controlling robot extremities. Cochlear implants.

Spencer raised an arm. Standing up, Commander Smith said, "Detective Spencer, I believe you have a question."

"Yes, thank you, sir. Witnesses have reported that when confronted by an escapee, they would suddenly stop, and tilt their head from side to side as if waiting for instructions. In your opinion, do you believe that the micro-stimulation electrode could have been controlled by a handler?"

"This is not my field of expertise. I am unable to comment if a boundary or noise would interfere with the signal being relayed back to a handler controlling the electrode. I know this isn't the answer you were expecting or hoping for," said the doctor.

Commander Smith once again stood up and said, "Please email me if you have questions in relation to what has been discussed today."

The meeting concluded at 2:30pm.

CHAPTER

21

There were no sirens blazing as the police approached the park. The constables introduced themselves to the woman who was clearly looking out for them.

"Helen?" Constable Stanley asked.

"Yes, Helen Poulos."

"Tell me what you found, Helen," Constable Stanley said.

"I was walking my dog Daisy. She pulled on her leash and started growling. As I got closer, I saw a man with silver skin. He moved slightly when I asked him if he was ok. I saw that there was a syringe in his arm. Then he stopped moving. Then I phoned 000."

Moving away from Helen, the constable spoke on her police radio, requesting collection of the body. The coroner's van arrived a few minutes later, to remove Dr Marinov's body.

"I'll need you to come to the police station and make a statement," the constable said.

"Of course, no problem. I'll take my dog home first and meet you there, if that's ok?" Helen asked.

"That's fine," replied Constable Stanley.

Driving to the station, Helen went over in her mind what Dr Marinov had said about not trusting the police. She gave her statement, not mentioning his recording on her phone.

Returning to her car, Helen's emotions took over. After a short cry, she turned the radio on and heard Michael Browne was on air. Dialling 131771, she spoke with a receptionist and asked if she could speak with Michael off air.

While waiting for Michael, an advertisement made her smile: "Need a criminal lawyer, call Brumpton Lawyers!"

"Michael Browne, how can I help you?"

"Hello, Michael. My name is Helen Poulos. Today at the park while walking my dog, I met Dr Alex Marinov. He asked if he could make a voice recording on my phone. He gave me instructions to give the recording to only you, Michael, and no one else."

"My radio segment finishes in 30 minutes. Come to the radio station and I'll meet you at reception," Michael said.

Arriving at the radio station, Helen went straight to reception.

"Hello, I'm Helen," she said nervously. "I have a meeting with Michael Browne."

"Yes, Michael said you would be popping by." The woman smiled and pointed to a room on the left. "Please wait here and Michael will join you shortly."

Helen waited only a few minutes before Michael joined her.

"I'm not sure how to start," she said.

"Let's start from the beginning. How do you know Dr Marinov?" the radio show host asked.

"I don't know him. I was walking my dog in the park earlier today, when she began growling. As I got closer, I saw a man with severe burns to his upper body lying on the ground.

"He told me who he was and asked if he could make a voice recording on my phone for you, and no-one else."

Sliding her phone across the table to Michael, Helen said, "The voice file is open. Just press play."

Michael pressed play and speaker. As he listened to his friend's voice, his demeanour changed. Tears began to run down his cheeks.

"Where is Alex now?" he asked.

"I'm sorry, Dr Marinov injected himself with a drug and died a few minutes after this was recorded," Helen said gently. "He asked me to call the police and report that I had found a body in the park. He told me not to trust the police. The police asked me to make a statement at the station. As promised, my statement was only that I found him while walking my dog Daisy."

"I have known Alex for a number of years. He was a brilliant man. I am proud to say he was my friend," said Michael.

Still visibly shaken by what he had heard on the recording, he asked, "May I take a copy of the recording?"

"Of course. That is what Dr Marinov wanted."

Michael made a copy of his friend speaking on Helen's phone. Then he thanked her and walked her to reception.

"Once this is out, and without compromising your statement to the police, would you return to the station and join me on my programme for an interview about this?"

"Yes, I would like that."

Handing her a card, Michael said, "This is my mobile number. If you want to talk, please call me."

He concluded their meeting with words that would stay with Helen for a long time: "Today is a very sad day!"

CHAPTER

22

Constable Stanley looked at her watch as she walked into the hospital reception area. Going over to the detectives, she said, "Great, we are all here. I've already confirmed Susan is in the left wing."

Standing at the nurse's station, Stanley asked if they could see Susan.

"Certainly. Susan is in bed 10," the nurse said.

Susan's eyes lit up when she saw Detective Walker walking towards her bed.

"Hello! Do you remember me?" he asked.

"You're the policeman from the underground house," she replied.

Understanding Susan was intellectually challenged, the detective said, "Yes, that is correct. Susan, do you mind if we talk about the underground house?"

"Dr Alex is my friend. Did he come with you?"

"No, he didn't. Has he come to visit you?" Walker asked.

Susan shook her head to indicate no.

Walker continued, "Do you know why you were at the underground house?"

"A man in a white coat said I was going on a holiday, but I didn't see anything. Why did he do that?" she asked.

"I am not sure. Did anyone hurt you?" he continued.

"Needles. I don't like needles. Dr Alex told them to stop," Susan said.

"Did they stop, Susan?" he asked.

"Yes, but they locked me in a room. I only got out to eat and go to the toilet. He said there was a man coming back for me."

"Who was coming back for you, Susan?"

"Agent Allan promised. He said he was going to make me better."

Susan yawned and the detective could see that she was tiring.

"We have to go now," he said.

"Will you come back to see me again?" she asked.

Knowing he couldn't let this girl get too attached to him, he said, "I'll try."

As they left the ward, Spencer asked the constable, "Where will Susan go when she is able to leave the hospital?"

"Not sure if she has family. I'll see if I can find out for you," she replied.

As they left the hospital, Spencer suddenly stopped. Watching a man entering the hospital he said, "that was the man acting suspiciously at the incident site," he said.

Stanley tapped Spencer on the shoulder and said, "Stay here. I'll follow him and see who he is visiting."

Walking straight past the nurse's workstation in the left wing, the visitor checked the board and saw that Susan was in bed 10.

Following the man, Stanley used her police hand radio. "Left wing, Susan!"

"Hello, Susan. Want to go for a drive?" the man asked the girl in bed 10.

Visibly distressed at seeing this new visitor, Susan cried out, "No!"

"Sir, you need to move away from the bed," Stanley commanded.

"No, she is coming with me."

"Move away from the bed," the police constable repeated.

Entering the wing, Walker and Spencer saw nurses starting to clear the ward.

Spencer walked over to the man and said, "I remember talking to you at the bunker site. Can I help you?"

Flicking open a pocket-knife and pointing it towards the detective, the man said, "The girl has to come with me."

"What's your name?"

"Norman."

"Norman, put the knife down."

Waving it around, Norman replied, "He won't pay me unless he has the girl."

Stanley distracted Norman so Spencer could grapple with him. The pocket-knife clattered to the floor. Spencer pushed the man face down before handcuffing him and escorting him out of the hospital. They drove him to the police station.

After Constable Stanley had read his rights to him at the police station, Norman said urgently, "I need to see the detective from the hospital!"

Stanley called out, "Detective Spencer, have you got a minute?"

"Yep," he said, coming to stand next to Stanley.

Tilting his head slightly towards the reception area, Norman yelled, "He won't pay me!"

Spencer turned around to see Special Agent Allan waiting in reception. Without uttering a word, the agent turned and left the station.

"Constable, please take Norman to a cell. Now, Constable!"

CHAPTER

23

Walker picked up his coffee cup as Spencer appeared at the door. They stared at each other for a moment. Then Spencer said, "We need to talk, but not here!"

Walker looked at him for a few seconds, opened his mouth slightly, then decided to not say anything. Instead, he walked out the back door, hoping that Spencer would follow.

Once the detectives were standing outside, Walker asked, "What's the look for, Spencer?"

"Norman, the guy we just brought into the station, identified Agent Allan as the man he claims won't pay him unless he gives him Susan!"

"What! Do you believe him?"

"Agent Allan looked extremely nervous as he left the station after Norman yelled that out."

Turning the police radio up, Walker and Spencer listened to a report about a disturbance at the Port Macquarie Base Hospital. They looked at each other.

Spencer said, "Susan!"

"You get the car and I'll tell the constable that we will follow her to the hospital," Walker said.

Following the convoy of police cars with flashing blue and red lights allowed them to arrive at the hospital within minutes.

As they rushed inside the hospital reception, the receptionist called out, "Left wing!"

It was chaotic in the left wing when they arrived, patients scurrying into rooms as nurses put the wing into lockdown.

The detectives went straight to bed 10. Walker cried out in anger as he realised Susan was gone.

A distressed nurse followed Walker. She said, "Three men in suits came to the wing, showed their ID, handcuffed her and took her."

Accessing his photos on his phone, Spencer showed the nurse a photo. "Was this one of the men?" he asked.

"Yes," she replied.

Looking at Walker he said, "Agent Allan!"

CHAPTER

24

"Good morning, listeners. I'm Michael Browne coming to you live from ABC North Coast Radio 771. Welcome to the programme. I have another busy show for you this morning.

"News headlines:

10-year-old sisters, Anna and Grace Fowler, reported missing at the Belltrees park, were found safe and well and have been reunited with their anxious parents.

"Continuing with the twins, looks like they befriended a midget in a costume. Reports are that Sasha, the twins' mother, found him hiding under their house.

"Cyclone Blake has been downgraded to a category 2. Residents near Pilbara have been advised to remain vigilant and stay indoors until the authorities give the all clear.

"Local man, sole winner of Thursday night Powerball, says it has set him and his family up for life.

"Now for an update on the Belltrees incident.

"Communications researcher Ella Murphy has been arrested and taken into custody. Did she start the fire at the Belltrees bunker?

"Police are remaining tight-lipped about the ME's report of the bodies found at the bunker site.

"Now for some sad news close to my heart. Close friend and scientist Dr Alex Marinov, working at the Belltrees bunker, was found deceased at the park. I do not have the full details surrounding his death, but my thoughts go out to his family at this sad time.

"My number is 131771, give me a call.

"Debbie has been waiting patiently on hold. Debbie, you are on air."

"Yesterday afternoon as I was leaving the Base Hospital after visiting my daughter, two police cars pulled up, no sirens but flashing lights, and three cops ran inside," Debbie said.

"I'll be having a catch-up with our news reporter Neville King at the top of the hour. Hopefully, he can give us an update on what happened at the Base Hospital, Debbie."

"Ryan, you are on the air."

"Sorry to hear about your friend, Michael."

"Thank you, Ryan."

"Um, the police haven't said anything more about what they found at the bunker site," continued Ryan. "Are we safe? Are my children safe? Look at the scare the Fowlers had when they couldn't find their children. Do you think that didn't cross their minds? I know we shouldn't speculate, but what if one of those tested people had taken the girls?"

"Yes, we shouldn't speculate, Ryan," Michael said.

"Stinks like a cover-up to me," Ryan said.

"Our news reporter Neville King is on the line. Neville, you have some breaking news?"

"Yes, Michael. The NSW Premier, Linda Porter, just held a press conference. She asked for a please explain why her government was not advised of the testing laboratory. The premier also asked for an update, as there are still subjects running loose in the community, and the state, for that matter. We heard the sad news about scientist Dr Alex Marinov. Lastly, the premier asked if the other scientists have been accounted for."

"Thanks, Neville.

"Well, there you have it, listeners. The premier has asked for a please explain.

"That's all from me today. I'm Michael Browne, ABC North Coast Radio 771. Enjoy the rest of your day."

CHAPTER

25

The meeting room was abuzz with detectives, local police and government official representatives when Area Commander Roger Smith entered the room.

"Ok, listen up! Your hard work has not gone unnoticed. Let's all meet here 9 o'clock tomorrow. Bring your notepads with you. Detectives Spencer and Walker, can you stay behind? Thanks."

After the room had emptied, Smith said, "You guys are doing a great job. Spencer, tell me what you know about Special Agent Allan."

"I first met Agent Allan when I was working private security detail at Pine Gap a few years ago. Not sure what his role was, but he always seemed to be standing beside the Minister for Defence, Melanie Grant."

"I know he removed Susan Tanner from the hospital. Just not sure where he is hiding her," the commander said. "I can't say very much as it is an ongoing investigation, but Agent Allan has been under suspicion of corruption for some time. Something happened in Pine Gap that the government needed to cover up. Four months ago, he was reassigned here to manage the experimentation bunker.

"You obviously are a threat to him, Detective Spencer. Agent Allan has asked that you be replaced with another detective. He is nervous with you being a member of this taskforce. But I don't take orders from ASIO agents!"

Turning to leave the room, he said, "I'll see you both tomorrow morning."

"Thank you, sir."

The detectives had started going through their files back at the police station when Constable Black approached Walker.

"Received anonymous phone call reporting a group of people hiding in an unused warehouse near Thrumster. The caller said a black SUV dropped them off about three days ago. Might be the missing scientists. I'm going to check it out. Want to tag along?" she asked.

Walker called out, "Would be better to take an unmarked car! Spencer, we might have a lead on the missing scientists."

"Right behind you," Spencer replied, as the three of them dashed out of the room.

"The location is in the old industrial area," Black said. "You guys know the area of Thrumster?"

"Nope," said Spencer.

"Thrumster, semi-rural, small acreage blocks. Perfect place to hide someone." Pulling over, she continued, "Up ahead 3 o'clock, black SUV, looks like a government car to me."

"Well, well," Walker said, passing binoculars to Spencer.

"If it isn't Agent Allan," Spencer said.

One by one, Agent Allan assisted men and women into the SUV. Still looking through the binoculars, Spencer said, "I count five scientists and four possible subjects, shit, including Susan Tanner."

Walker quickly took photos of Agent Allan escorting each person from the warehouse to the SUV.

"Do you want to call it in?" Black asked.

"No, let's keep following them and see where they go," Spencer said.

Keeping a good distance behind the SUV, Constable Black followed the vehicle for about 4 kilometres. The SUV stopped at another unused property, this time an old motel near Port Macquarie Airport.

"Fuck!" Walker said again, passing the binoculars to Spencer.

"Commander Roger Smith! Looks like the North Coast Police Department may be involved," muttered Spencer.

"I think we need to make a call to our Area Commander, Phillip Morgan. You with us, Black?" Walker asked.

"Absolutely! Not all police officers on the North Coast are crooked."

CHAPTER

26

Detective Walker phoned his superior, Area Commander Phillip Morgan, when they arrived back at the station.

"Good afternoon, sir. It's Peter Walker here. I have you on speaker phone. With me are Joe Spencer and local Constable Alice Black."

"Commander Roger Smith tells me you guys have fitted in well with the team."

"Speaking of the investigation, we have a few concerns, sir," Spencer said.

"I have been getting briefs since the investigation commenced. Tell me what your concerns are," the commander said.

"We interviewed one of the survivors, a young woman named Susan Tanner. Susan's file identified her as being slightly intellectually challenged, and that's why she was chosen. As we were leaving the hospital, a man who I briefly spoke with at the incident site was entering the hospital. He wanted to know where they took Susan.

"Inside the hospital, the man armed himself with a pocket-knife. After a short struggle, he was apprehended. He kept repeating over and over that he wouldn't get paid if he didn't take Susan.

"Later at the police station, he indicated the man he was referring to. At that time there were only three people in clear view that he could see: Constable Stanley, myself and Special Agent Allan."

"Constable Black here, sir. Earlier today, we received an anonymous tip about people hiding out in the old industrial region near Thrumster. Detectives Walker and Spencer accompanied me to the address where we saw Agent Allan assisting people into an SUV. Once leaving this address, we followed the SUV for about 4 kilometres, where he dropped

them off at an unused motel. Area Commander Roger Smith was waiting at this site."

"Hell! Have you spoken to anyone else about this?" Morgan asked.

"No, sir," they all replied.

"Good, keep it that way. Stay at the police station. I'm leaving now. Detectives and Constable Black, good work!" he concluded.

"Can we trust him?" Constable Black asked.

"I have worked with Morgan for four years. We can trust him," Walker assured her. "We can't let anyone know we spoke with Commander Morgan today."

Spencer and Black both nodded their heads.

"Ok, let's go back and continue work," Black said.

CHAPTER
27

Detectives Walker and Spencer were sitting in an interview room when Constable Black wheeled in an electronic whiteboard.

"Ok, let's start from the beginning and see what we have found out so far," she said.

They read the following:

Bunker site

- Communications Researcher Ella Murphy called 000 reporting a fire at the Bunker site

- Bushwalkers Tom and Harrison Walters came across a manhole and opened it

- The "robot on fire," who turned out to be Dr Alex Marinov, jumped out of the manhole

- A number of scientists and subjects escaped via the manhole

- Lead scientist Dr Phillip Anderson assisted police by identifying the two bodies outside the bunker as two subjects

- Subject, Susan Tanner, found alive, was taken to hospital

- Ella Murphy, driving away from the bunker, saw Tom and his son Harrison running through bush, picked them up and drove them to town

- Two bodies were taken to the Port Macquarie Base Hospital Forensic Medicine Division, ME Dr Raelene Attard, did an autopsy on the bodies

- Two scientists, Dr Ben Fullwood and Dr Tony Weller, identified as deceased at the bunker site

- Scott Kelly was possibly a security guard at the bunker

- Dr Alex Marinov, running through the bush, pushed Kerry Taylor to the ground

- Subject Barney befriended twins Anna and Grace at a park. Anna and Grace then hid Barney under their house. Barney is now in custody

- Hiker Matt Peters found Kerry Taylor disorientated and covered in mud. Assisted her to safety

- Subject identified as Gavin escaped the fire and ran into the bush, hiding in an abandoned cabin

- Matt helped Kerry to the same cabin. They were confronted by Gavin, who hit Matt on the head with an axe handle and was holding Kerry as a hostage in the cabin

- Helen Poulos found Dr Alex Marinov deceased in the park whilst walking her dog

- Detectives Walker and Spencer entered the cabin. Gavin was armed with an axe, lunged towards Spencer, who used his taser to immobilise and handcuff him

- Detectives Walker and Spencer interviewed Ella Murphy. Ella admitted to taking files

- Constable Black, Detectives Walker and Spencer visited Port Macquarie Base Hospital and spoke with Susan Tanner

- Norman Fitzgerald, seen at the bunker, also entered the hospital

- Normal Fitzgerald went to Susan Tanner's room

- When confronted, Norman pulled out a pocket-knife. He surrendered, was handcuffed and taken to the police station

- Norman Fitzgerald identified Special Agent Allan (also at the police station) as the person who wouldn't pay him if he didn't bring Susan to him

- Constable Black, Detectives Walker and Spencer responded to an anonymous phone call about people staying in an old industrial area

- Area Commander Roger Smith advised that Agent Allan has been under surveillance for some months, on suspicion of corruption

- Agent Allan helped what looked like scientists and subjects into an SUV and relocated the passengers to an old derelict motel

- North Coast Area Commander Roger Smith met the vehicle and ushered the occupants of the SUV into a motel room

"That's it in a nutshell!" Spencer exclaimed.

"I'm going to save this on a USB, print three copies, then delete the contents from the board," Black said.

As Constable Black gave both Walker and Spencer a copy of the summary and the USB, she said, "By the way, I checked Agent Allan's car registration, registered private. As I just happened to have a GPS tracker in my pocket, I put it beneath the undercarriage near the rear wheel wells of his SUV. That's my shift done. I need a drink. Any takers?" she asked.

Walker and Spencer couldn't help but smile as Walker said, "You deserve a drink after that. Let's go!"

CHAPTER

28

NSW Police Commissioner Warren Davies's office was on the fourth floor. Arriving at Police Headquarters, Area Commander Phillip Morgan opened his car door as he dialled the commissioner's telephone number.

"Good morning, sir. Phillip Morgan here. Wondering if we could have a quick chat this morning."

"I'm free this morning. Why don't you pop by my office?"

"On my way," Morgan replied.

Commissioner Davies didn't like the glamour of expensive furniture. His office was sparse – modern, but sparse.

After going through security, Phillip Morgan presented himself at the commissioner's office and said, "Area Commander Phillip Morgan here to see the Police Commissioner!"

"Phillip, come in," the commissioner said, as he opened the door of his office Shaking hands, Morgan said, "Sorry to barge in!"

"No apologies necessary. What can I do for you?"

The sun was bright as it glistened off the adjacent building's windows. Morgan shifted position so that the glare was not so much in his eyes.

"You are obviously aware of the Belltrees bunker fire earlier in the week. Have you had much to do with the operation at the bunker?"

"Yes, I am aware of the project and the tragic fire that has occurred."

"So, you knew the bunker was experimenting on people, or, as they call them, subjects?" Morgan asked. "Did you also know that ASIO is involved?"

The commissioner's annoyance was evident by the tone of his voice as he replied. "Yes, I knew of the trial experiments that were being conducted at the bunker site. What I am about to tell you is confidential, Morgan. The Federal Police and ASIO have been conducting a joint investigation. Special Agent Allan has been under investigation for some time."

The room went quiet for a moment before Morgan spoke. "Sir, with respect, I would have thought that before I was to send two of my detectives to join the taskforce, I would have been briefed on these experiments. Lives have been lost, and some of the subjects, as they call them, have escaped and have been terrifying the small community of Belltrees!

"I am heading up to Port Macquarie this afternoon, but before I leave, I would like to have access to the Bunker Experimentation file," he said.

Seconds passed before the commissioner replied. "It's short notice but let me see what I can do. Oh, and Morgan, when you arrive at Port Macquarie, your presence may be treated as intrusive. Remember, you are an observer only. It is not your case," the commissioner said, as he closed the door behind the commander.

CHAPTER

29

It was right on 4 o'clock when Special Agent Allan arrived at Helen's home.

Allan flashed his badge as he introduced himself. "Good afternoon. My name is Special Agent Allan. You're Helen, correct?"

"Yes, I am Helen, Special Agent Allan. Am I in trouble?" she asked.

"Not at all, but I would like to speak with you about the day you found the man in the park. Is it ok if I come in?"

"Yes, sorry, how rude of me. Please come in," Helen said, as she moved aside for him to enter the house.

She showed the agent into the living room. "Can I get you a cup of tea or maybe coffee?"

"No, I am fine," replied the agent.

"You said you wanted to speak with me about the man in the park. How can I help you?" Helen asked.

"In your statement, you said the man was already deceased. Is that correct?" he asked.

"Yes, that is correct."

"You didn't touch the body. Didn't take anything out of his pockets?" he asked.

Shocked by the question, Helen replied, "Of course not!"

"Did you know the man, Helen?"

"No, I didn't know him."

"Do you watch the news, Helen? You have probably seen on the news that he was one of the scientists working in the bunker. He didn't, by any chance, give you anything, did he, Helen?"

"No, as I told the police, he was already dead."

"Did you notice anything strange about the man, the way the body was lying, as if someone had perhaps searched him before your dog Daisy found him?" he asked.

"He certainly didn't look like a scientist. I thought he was a clown at first, you know, because of the silver skin. If it wasn't for my dog Daisy barking, I wouldn't have come across him at all."

Passing Helen a business card, Special Agent Allan said, "If you remember anything else, please phone me."

Just as the agent was leaving, Helen's mobile rang. Seeing the caller ID, she hesitated to answer. It rang again.

"You going to answer that?" he said.

She glanced at the ID again. Answering, she said, "Hello, Mary. How are you? I have visitors at the moment. Can I phone you back? Yes, I will be free in about half an hour. I'll talk to you then, Mary."

"You look upset. Everything ok, Helen?"

"Yes, thank you," she said, as she closed the door.

CHAPTER

30

Helen stood still for a while before she decided that she would phone Michael Browne.

Using her late husband's android phone, Helen messaged Michael's number.

Hi Michael, it's Helen. Please phone me back on this number.

Seconds later, the phone rang.

"Michael?"

"Yes, it's me, Helen. Is everything ok?"

"Sorry about before. I had a visit from, actually, I don't know where he was from, but he called himself Special Agent Allan."

"Who owns this number?"

"My late husband. I just can't let it go yet. Perhaps I watch too much TV. Thought he might be tracing my calls or something."

Chuckling softly, Michael asked, "What did he want?"

"He asked me about Dr Marinov. Did I move his body or did I remove anything from his body?"

"I'm still at the radio station preparing my next on-air broadcast. You sound a bit startled. Would you like to come over?"

"Yes, I was hoping you would say that," she replied.

About thirty minutes later, Helen walked into the radio station. Michael was waiting at reception.

"Let's go into the tearoom."

They both spoke at the same time.

"Please, you first," Michael said.

"Why would a special agent be visiting me?" she asked.

Moving to his laptop, Michael pulled up a page. "I did some checking. Special Agent Allan is an ASIO agent. He is on the taskforce assigned to work on the Belltrees incident."

"Before Dr Marinov died, he gave me a key to a safety deposit box. He told me to keep it in a safe place," Helen said. "He also told me not to tell you right now, but after what happened this afternoon, I felt I needed to talk to you."

"Don't betray Alex's trust. You tell me when you are ready," said Michael.

"Funny, Dr Marinov said the same thing, that I will know when the time is right to talk to you about it. Do you think the agent knew about the safety deposit box? Maybe he knew I had the key. This is freaking me out now."

Michael patted her on the arm. "Stay here for as long as you need. I'm going to do some digging and see if I can find anything else out."

CHAPTER

31

Constable Black impatiently tapped her fingers on the desk as she waited for Detectives Walker and Spencer to arrive at the police station.

"Finally!" she said, as they both entered the front door of the station.

"Checked the GPS tracker I put under Agent Allan's car this morning. He visited the usual spots: the hotel where he is staying, the local pub. Two other destinations he visited caught my attention.

"He visited a woman named Helen Poulos, who had reported a body in the park. That body was Dr Alex Marinov.

"Tom and Harrison Walters said they were chased by a robot on fire through the bush," she continued. "I checked Tom Walters's statement. Fairly straightforward: bushwalking and came across a bunker manhole.

"I was on duty when Helen came in to make a statement. Widow, husband died a year or so back. As far as I can tell, she did not know Dr Marinov or the Walters family."

"What was the second one?" Walker asked.

"Ella Murphy. The GPS showed he was at this location for over an hour."

Checking the system, Constable Black announced, "Ok, Agent Allan is on the move again, heading west towards the airport. The sergeant has me working desk duty today. Here is the tracker if you want to know what Agent Allan is up to."

The door to the detectives' office swung open. Sergeant Parker said, "Constable Black, you're on desk duty today. What are you waiting for!"

Black took a deep breath before standing up. "Got it, Sergeant!"

"Sorry, Sergeant. The constable has been invaluable to us with her local knowledge," Walker said.

"Constable Black is a good police officer, enthusiastic and willing to help," the sergeant replied.

Walker checked the GPS. "Looks like Agent Allan is heading towards the airport. Let's go see what he is up to."

Walker pulled up in a deserted street at the back of the airport and kept a safe distance from Agent Allan's parked SUV.

Looking through binoculars, Spencer said, "I can see movement up ahead past where the SUV is parked."

Turning to face Walker, he said, "Why would a security detail be walking people from the motel and into what looks like an army vehicle?"

Looking through the binoculars again, he then said, "Wait a minute, these aren't the scientists and subjects we saw two days ago. They're gone! This is a decoy!"

CHAPTER

32

It was one in the afternoon when Area Commander Roger Smith walked into the Port Macquarie Police Station. Slamming the door as he entered made everyone look up.

"Sergeant Parker, has Constable Black commenced her shift yet?"

"No, Commander. Constable Black commences her shift at two. Can I assist you?" he asked.

"Is Detective Walker currently in the station?"

"Yes, Commander. Detective Walker is here, sir."

Walker knew Commander Smith was not one to cross. Walking into his office, he said, "Commander, you were asking for me?"

"Yes, Detective. Commander Morgan is on his way up here. You know anything about this?"

"No, sir," he replied.

"Ok, that's all," he replied, as he left the station, slamming the door again as he left.

Sergeant Parker's superior was already out the door when he asked Detective Walker, "What's got up his nose today?"

"No idea," he replied.

"The coffee boy has arrived," Detective Spencer said, as he started handing out the coffees.

Giving Walker his cup, Spencer said, "Just saw Commander Smith outside speaking with what looked a couple of feds. The only sentence I heard was, 'Do you think they suspect?'"

"Fuck! Commander Smith asked me if I knew why Commander Morgan was on his way up here."

Before Walker could say another word, the station door opened and Commander Smith said to Parker, "I'll be at the helipad if anyone is looking for me. Detectives, you're with me."

The ride to the helipad was tense, no words spoken.

CHAPTER

33

It felt like time had stopped at the airport as Area Commander Murphy, and Detectives Spencer and Walker waited for Commander Morgan to step off the helicopter.

A voice came over the police radio, "Commander Morgan's helicopter has just arrived!" Opening the car door, Commander Murphy made his way across the helipad.

"Welcome, Phillip. Good to see you again," Commander Murphy greeted him.

Extending his hand, Commander Morgan said, "Ronald, good to see you too."

"My car is over here. Walker and Spencer are in the car and will be joining us," he said, pointing to the edge of the helipad.

"Detectives. Reports are that you have been invaluable assets for the investigation," Morgan said, as he opened the car door.

"Let's go to my office for a debriefing," Murphy said.

The building garage was almost empty when their car pulled into the driveway and entered the underground carpark.

"Would you like us to stay?" asked Walker.

"Yes," Murphy said, as he looked to Morgan for approval.

"By all means," Morgan said.

"I met with the Police Commissioner Davies earlier today," he continued. "We discussed the Belltrees incident and he confirmed that he knew about the trial experiments being conducted."

"What's this really about, Phillip? Why are you really here?"

Morgan was being careful not to put too many cards on the table. He didn't know if the Police Commissioner had told him about their impromptu meeting earlier in the day.

"Have you located the remaining five scientists and four subjects?" he asked.

Turning his questions to his detectives, he asked, "Detectives, do you know the whereabouts of the missing scientists and subjects?"

"No, sir. The scientists' vehicles were abandoned and left in the bunker carpark. They had help in escaping not only the fire but also the area following the fire. We can only assume that the surviving subjects and scientists are together," Spencer said. "We have only been able to interview a non-tested subject survivor, 16-year-old Susan. Unfortunately, Susan has disappeared."

"The media are having a field day, allegations that the government had sponsored the whole project including the fire, due to unsuccessful results," said Morgan. "One last request, if I may, full access to all the case files. Walker and Spencer can bring me up to speed as we review them."

"Yes. Detectives, the files will be on your desks in the morning," Murphy said.

"I'm staying at Port Macquarie for a couple of days. Ronald, let's have another catch-up before I leave."

Morgan ended their conversation by requesting a car to collect himself and his detectives.

Once all three men were in the car, Commander Morgan said, "I did a bit of digging before I left Sydney, and I am sure Commander Murphy is aware of that now. Oh, and by the way, you're shouting drinks tonight, Detectives!"

CHAPTER
34

It was late afternoon when Agent Allan pulled into Ella Murphy's driveway.

As the doorbell sounded, Ella asked, "Special Agent Allan, what brings you to my door?"

"Do you mind if I come in?"

Unlocking the screen door, Ella invited the agent inside.

With a smile on his face, the agent said, "Something smells nice!"

"I've just made a batch of muffins. Would you like coffee and muffin?"

"Unfortunately, this isn't a social call. I am following up on a development in the bunker fire. Do you live on your own, Ella?"

"Yes. This was a new start for me. I moved from the city."

"On the day of the fire, did you take anything from the bunker?"

"Yes, my colleague Scott gave me some files and asked me to keep them safe."

"Where are those files now, Ella?"

"I gave them to Detective Spencer the day he and Detective Walker interviewed me. Should I be worried? Am I under arrest?"

Ignoring her question, Allan asked, "Did you open the files?"

"No!"

"I think I will have that muffin, if the offer still stands, Ella?"

Ella stuttered when she was nervous. Walking towards the kitchen, she said, "C-c-certainly."

Putting on a pair of latex gloves, Allan followed Ella to the kitchen.

Quickly, he pinned her against the fridge. He then placed a plastic bag over her head.

Trinkets fell off the fridge door and scattered across the floor.

Fear overtook Ella. Her breathing was rapid as she said, "Please, you don't have to do this."

"Now, now, don't fight it."

It took about two minutes before Ella lost consciousness. Allan tied the bag securely around her neck and carefully laid her on the floor before he walked through the house looking for something to conceal the body.

"This will do," he said, as he pulled a blanket off a bed and returned to the kitchen and to Ella's lifeless body.

All he needed to do now was wait until dark when he could safely remove the body.

He sat quietly in the loungeroom and read his messages, before making the call to report that the job was done.

Darkness had fallen by the time the clock in the loungeroom chimed six times. He used the car remote to release the boot as he opened the front door, and checked no-one was around, before carefully picking up the blanket and leaving the house.

The drive to Port Macquarie took about three hours. He dumped the body at Settlement Point.

Allan's demeanour and arrogance were obvious even to himself. He knew he had a psychopathic personality.

He was a killer!

CHAPTER

35

"Where are the case photos?" Walker asked.

Handing them to Walker, Spencer said, "What's on your mind?"

"Remember Ella identified Scott in one of the photos we showed her? I don't remember seeing him in the photos we took at the industrial area, you know, where Allan was loading the survivors into his SUV!"

Laying the photos on the desk, the detectives confirmed that Scott Kelly was not in any of the photos.

"Don't you think it's strange? He wasn't one of the deceased at the fire and he isn't in the photos."

Walker put his head around the corner and called out, "Constable, do you have an address for the bunker security officer, Scott Kelly?"

After checking the database, Black walked into the office and said, "Sure do, 22 Arthur Street, Port Macquarie."

Observing Walker looking at the photos, she asked, "Find something?"

"Yes and no. Ella identified Scott was the security person at the bunker. We know he survived the fire, but he doesn't appear to be in any of these photos of the survivors that we took at the industrial site."

"Do you think Allan had an accomplice?"

Raising an eyebrow, Walker said, "Spencer, Constable Black and I are going to pay Mr Kelly a visit."

After they had been on the road for about half an hour, Black said, "Take the next right, then the first left should be Arthur Street. There it is, number 22, the big white house."

"Well, someone is home. Listen to that racket. Surprised someone hasn't complained about the volume of the music."

Black turned to Walker, "What is that smell?"

Instead of knocking, Black battered down the door to gain access.

"Mr Kelly, it's Constable Black from Port Macquarie Police Station."

It didn't take too long before they could see where the smell was coming from. Mr Kelly's decomposing body was lying on the loungeroom floor. With gloves on,

Walker turned the music off.

There were no obvious signs of foul play.

"I'll call it in," Black said.

Removing her two-way radio from its holster, she clicked the speaker button and said, "This is Constable Black. Deceased male at 22 Arthur Street, Port Macquarie. We need ME and forensics!"

Not wanting to disturb the possible crime scene, Walker and Black returned to their car and waited for the ME to arrive.

CHAPTER

36

Benjamin White nervously approached the Port Macquarie Police Station front desk.

Standing behind the counter, Constable Black said, "Good morning, sir. How can I help you?"

"I need to speak with Detective Walker."

"May I ask what it is in relation to, sir?"

"My name is Benjamin White. I was working in the Belltrees bunker."

"Take a seat, sir. I'll let the detective know you are here."

Black saw Detective Walker standing in the corridor towards the back of the station and raised her arm to beckon him to approach her.

"Sorry to interrupt your meeting with Commander Morgan. There is a man named Benjamin White at the front desk who said he worked in the Belltrees bunker. He specifically asked for you."

Raising his eyebrows to show his interest, Walker thanked her and made his way back to Detective Spencer and Commander Morgan.

"Spencer, can you search a name in the system, Benjamin White?" Walker asked.

"Not in the system," Spencer replied after a few minutes.

Walker said, "He is in the waiting room, has asked for me and said he worked in the Belltrees bunker. I'll go get him and meet you in interview room 2, Spencer."

At the front desk, Walker met the constable who said, "This is one nervous man. He is sitting in the corner."

"Benjamin, I'm Detective Walker," said the detective, trying to sound as friendly as possible. Let's go somewhere quiet for a chat."

Following Walker, Benjamin entered the interview room.

"I've asked Detective Spencer to join us," said Walker.

"Ok," said the man, almost in a whisper.

"How can we help you today, Benjamin?" asked Walker.

Wiping his brow, the man nervously said, "I worked in the Belltrees bunker. I was the handler of a subject named Gavin.

"Gavin has a tracking device implanted in his wrist. After the fire, I tracked him to a cabin. Watching from the trees, I saw a man and an injured woman enter the cabin. Not long after that, I saw both of you also enter the cabin. I heard some yelling, and you took Gavin away in handcuffs. I continued tracking him. He was brought to this police station."

"Why didn't you come forward before now, Benjamin?" Walker asked.

"The agent told me I would be in trouble. He told me to lay low for a few days."

"How did the agent contact you? Did you ever meet the agent?" Spencer asked.

"I saw him at the bunker a couple of times, but he always contacted me on my mobile."

Taking photos from an envelope, Walker said, "I am going to show three photos. Have you met any of these men? Take your time."

He laid the photos on the table. Without hesitation, Benjamin tapped on the photo of Special Agent Allan.

"That's him!"

Picking up another photo, Benjamin said, "Scott, um, Scott Kelly. I think he may have been a security guard. He came in every morning and left before nightfall on weekdays."

Pointing to the photo of Agent Allan, Spencer asked, "Have you had contact with this man you have identified since you tracked Gavin here?"

"Yes, he gave me an address where he told me Gavin, two other subjects and some scientists were being taken. He said it was an old motel. He called it a safe house."

"Does this man know that Gavin has a tracking device implanted in his wrist and that you can track him?" Spencer asked.

"No, I don't think so," Benjamin replied.

"It is extremely important that you tell no one about this tracker," Detective Spencer said.

"Yes, I understand," was the reply.

Standing up, Walker said, "Thank you for coming in, Benjamin. This is my contact number. If the agent contacts you again or if you see that Gavin is on the move, please phone me."

"I understand. Thank you, Detective." Benjamin looked nervously around the room before he spoke again. "On the day of the fire, Agent Allan was in the underground bunker. He told all personnel the experiment was being shut down. He threw a Molotov cocktail into one of the living quarters, which then engulfed the bunker in a raging fire."

CHAPTER

37

Area Commander Morgan was having breakfast with Detectives Walker and Spencer when the call came over the radio, the operator saying, "Female body found floating in the Hastings River near Settlement Point!"

Morgan looked at Walker and Spencer and said, "I can get to the helipad. This may be related to the case. Go!"

"Thank you," they both replied.

"I'll expect an updated report on my desk tomorrow morning," Morgan added.

Heading towards the car, Sergeant Parker dialled Walker's mobile number.

Not recognising the number, Walker answered, "Detective Walker."

"Good morning, Detective. It's Sergeant Parker. Did you hear the call on the radio about the body in the river?"

"Good morning, Sergeant. You're on speaker and yes, we did."

"Do you know who called it in?" Spencer asked.

"Female, anonymous, but whoever she was, she sounded shaken, spooked."

"Ok, meet you there in 10 minutes," Walker said.

By the time the detectives got to the crime scene, television crews were already there. A makeup artist was applying makeup to an attractive brunette as she gave instructions to the cameraman about where to set up.

Officers were directing the crowd that had gathered away from the police tape and the crime scene.

Sergeant Parker called out as he saw the detectives exiting their car.

Showing their police badges to the local police, the sergeant said, "The detectives are with me!

"The body has already been retrieved from the water by forensics," he said. The woman who found her was shaken up."

Detective Walker put his head down as he turned away from the body.

"We don't know it's her," Spencer remarked.

"You know this woman?" Parker asked.

The sergeant was about to ask another question when a forensic officer approached the trio and said, "Tim Mathers. I examined the body once it was retrieved from the water. Looks to be around 18-25 years old, probably been in the water between 6-10 hours. Initial indications show asphyxiation, head was in a plastic bag. There are bluish bruises on the face which can occur after death. I will be able to confirm cause and time of death at the autopsy."

Handing his business card to Tim Mathers, Walker said, "Take my card and phone me when you have more information on the body."

"When I get back to the station, I will check to see if someone has reported a missing woman," the sergeant said. "For now, she will be tagged as Jane Doe."

CHAPTER

38

"Good morning, listeners. I'm Michael Browne, coming to you live from ABC North Coast Radio 771. Welcome to the programme. I have another busy show for you this morning.

"News headlines:

A 3.1 magnitude earthquake struck Christchurch overnight. Residents have reported waking up to houses shaking for about 10-15 seconds. No reports of loss of life or damage to buildings.

Two men charged after counter terrorism unit raided a house in western Sydney.

Heavy fog coated Sydney this morning, causing visibility of less than 500 metres.

"Now to local news:

A young woman's body found floating in the Hastings River near Settlement Point.

A man was found deceased at his home in Port Macquarie.

Formal identification has not been made yet.

"Let's go to our news reporter Neville King for an update.

"Good morning, Neville. Two bodies in two days!"

"Yes, police haven't indicated if they believe these findings are linked. A young woman in her early twenties was found floating in the Hastings River. First reports are that a bag was found over her head. A crime scene has been set up. No formal ID has been made.

"Decomposing body of a man in his thirties, found at his home. First reports are that it's a possible drug overdose. No formal ID has been made."

"Thanks, Neville.

"Now it's your turn listeners. My number is 131771, give me a call."

"Ted, I believe you and your wife Olga are celebrating your 50th wedding anniversary today. I also hear you have a funny story as to how you first met Olga."

"Yes, Michael. When I was 18, I did a paper run for my uncle. Every afternoon, a very sweet young girl waited by her gate to catch the paper as I threw it in her yard. I made up my mind that one day I would hop off my bike, hand her the paper and invite her to the movies.

Well, that day came, but instead of hopping off my bike, I fell off and the papers scattered everywhere. That was our first date. Six months later, we married. We have two boys, both married, and five beautiful grandchildren. Today we are celebrating our 50th wedding anniversary."

"What a wonderful story, Ted. Happy 50th wedding anniversary, Olga and Ted.

"Let's take another call. Alice you're on the air. I believe you have a story about your dog."

"Yep, little Bella. I was sitting on my front veranda one day eating a hamburger when a skinny little dog sat down beside me. She didn't beg for food, just sat beside me. Hoping she wouldn't bite, I picked her up and took her inside. Bella is now four and my fur baby. We still sit on the veranda. She's always quick to hop on my lap for cuddles."

"Another wonderful story. Bella sounds like one lucky dog.

"Well, that's all we have time for today. I'm Michael Browne, ABC North Coast Radio 771. Enjoy the rest of your day."

CHAPTER
39

On Thursday morning, Area Commander Morgan arrived at headquarters and headed towards his office on the fifth floor to find the Police Commissioner, Warren Davies sitting at his desk looking out the window.

"Good morning, sir," Morgan said, as he entered the office.

"Phillip, I just had a call from the head of ASIO. We have a rogue agent; Agent Allan was suspended last week and hasn't been sighted since being stood down," Davies said.

"The bunker experiment has been canned and all bunkers have been shut down. The scientists and participants have remained locked up in their bunkers for their own protection."

"I also heard the surviving scientists and participants from the Belltrees bunker have gone missing. Let's hope it's not at the handiwork of Allan," the Commissioner concluded.

"They were being kept at an old motel near Port Macquarie, then they just disappeared. The local police are canvassing the area. Walker and Spencer are still working with local police. I am due for an update this afternoon," Morgan said.

"Sir, I think it would have been prudent for all law enforcement agencies to have been advised about the bunker experiments," Morgan said.

"As we speak," said the commissioner, "the police are raiding Agent Allan's house, looking for clues of where he might have gone."

Morgan's secretary buzzed through. "Commander Morgan, there is a call on hold for the Police Commissioner."

The commissioner reached over the desk and pressed line 3 and speaker. He seemed to know who the call would be from. "Blackburn, you are on speaker. What do you have for me?"

"Sir, I am at Agent Allan's place. There is some serious stuff here. I've just sent you a photo of a map of Australia I found."

Opening his messages, the commissioner and Morgan looked at a map, as Blackburn said, "Firstly, the red cross: this is an address circled in Canberra, labelled Warby Laboratory. This could be where they make the hardware that has been surgically implanted in each participant. Secondly, you will see six circles. I have discovered each of these circles are the locations of all the bunkers, including the bunker at Belltrees. From the intel I have collected here, I believe the participants were held on a boat, and once they had their implants and began their transition to their new persona, they were put in trucks and driven to each bunker to continue their experiments.

"Sir, there are more than 20 printed emails scattered on the table, emails from some very important people from our law enforcement agencies.

"I am going to pack this up, hand it in to headquarters and put it in the lockup. This information cannot go missing, sir."

"Good work, Blackburn. Round it up and get the hell out there."

As the commissioner left Morgan's office, he said, "An APB has been put out for Agent Allan. I'll keep you updated."

CHAPTER

40

Gary Fernley, AFP Commissioner, was chairing an emergency meeting with all the law enforcement agency heads.

"Gentlemen, in front of you is an update on the Belltrees bunker investigation. I have also invited Senior Detective Paul Blackburn, who was the lead in the raid at Agent Allan's residence."

Commissioner Fernley pressed a button on his phone.

"Yes, sir?"

"Please send in Blackburn."

A middle-aged man stepped into the office and sat down opposite the commissioner, as he introduced him to all present.

"Paul, bring us up to speed in regards the raid on Agent Allan's residence."

"If I can firstly take a step back. Agent Allan has had a history of depression following the incident where he, in a drunken state, ran over his daughter a few years ago.

Records show he became reckless following the accident. His daughter Susan survived, suffered a brain injury, cognitive behaviour being impaired.

"Allan confided in a fellow agent that he was determined to make his daughter better. When he heard about the secret experimentation bunkers, he asked that his daughter be selected as a candidate.

"Allan was transferred from Pine Gap to head the newly formed human medical experiment programme. Other than Susan, it isn't clear how the subjects were selected. Most of them had either criminal backgrounds or mental issues. It is believed that these were non-consensual experiments."

"Holy fuck," Fernley said.

Blackburn clicked a remote and a screen appeared in front of the group.

"The documents in front of you are what I collected from Allan's residence."

He clicked again and three photos appeared on the screen.

"A boat named Opportunities is currently anchored 400 kilometres from Sydney, 2 kilometres off the Australian coast, in the Port Macquarie area. With the assistance of Border Force, a defence drone using heat censors determined that the boat is currently unoccupied, possibly abandoned.

"Border Force boarded Opportunities an hour ago. This boat has been fitted with an operating theatre, equipped with what would be used for minor surgeries. There are four enclosures separated by thick glass. It is believed that the subjects were operated on on the mainland, then transported to the boat. At this stage, it isn't clear whether they were shipped to the bunkers around the country or relocated by road on trucks. This is still under investigation.

"All bunkers have been closed, and subjects and scientists have been relocated to a safe house.

"One subject is missing from the Belltrees bunker – Susan!"

CHAPTER

41

It was dark by the time Walker and Spencer arrived at their hotel and parked their car in the underground parking area. Walker always preferred to leave his room key at the lobby, not that he had much in his room, but it was a routine that he had followed for years.

"I'll see you at dinner," Spencer said, as Walker exited the lift at the lobby.

Walker replied slowly. "Yeah, see you at dinner." He was musing about whether they had let Ella down.

The room was warm. He felt there wasn't the need to put on the air conditioner as he undressed and showered, before changing into a casual pair of jeans and shirt.

An old rock and roll song made his phone start vibrating on the bedside table. He said to himself, *perhaps it is time for a more updated song!*

As he picked up the phone, before he could say his name, a panicky male voice said, "Detective, it's Benjamin

White. You told me to contact you if Gavin's tracker alerted me of movement."

"Take a breath, Benjamin, and tell me where you are."

"I followed the tracker and it stopped at that old motel that the agent called the safe house."

"Stay in your car. We are coming to you. Do not go into the safe house."

Spencer answered his mobile after the first ring. "Miss me already, Walker!"

"Benjamin White just contacted me. Gavin's tracker alerted a movement. He is at the safe house. I'll call Constable Black for backup."

"Meet me at the lift," Spencer replied.

As the detectives drove towards the safe house Spencer received a text from Commander Morgan advising that Agent Allan was a rogue agent and an APB had been issued for his arrest.

"Shit! An APB has been issued for Allan's arrest!" he said.

A block away from the address, Walker handed his phone to Spencer and said, "Dial my last call from the log. Hopefully, Benjamin hasn't tried to be a hero."

Constable Black and two other constables arrived at the safe house.

Walker asked them, "Did you get the message that an APB has been issued on Allan?"

Turning on his earpiece, Spencer took the lead and instructed the constables to go around the back. He and Walker stood beside a front window.

Spencer spoke. "Four civilians are on the west side of the front room and Agent Allan is standing on the northwest side. He is armed with a small calibre pistol in his holster and another on his lower right leg."

"Ready?" Walker asked his partner.

"Yep!"

Using his fingers, he counted down from five before Spencer kicked in the door. Walker called out, "Police, don't move, don't move!"

Constable Black kicked in the back door at the same time.

All three police officers pointed their glocks in the direction of Allan.

"Detectives, everything is under control and the survivors are safe," Allan said. He looked from one of them to the other. "What's wrong? I told you the survivors are safe."

"Slowly, remove your holster," Walker said.

Allan opened his jacket to reveal a glock in his holster. He reluctantly released it and handed it over to Walker.

As Walker pulled Allan's hands behind his back, he said, "Agent Allan, you are under arrest for the alleged kidnapping of bunker personnel and the suspected murder of Ella Murphy."

"I don't see Susan. Where is Susan?" Spencer asked.

"Who?" said Allan.

Dr Phillip Anderson stepped forward and said, "The girl isn't here. Benjamin was here two days ago and returned yesterday. He removed the tracker from Gavin's wrist. He returned about an hour ago. He seemed to be in a rush. He kept saying they had to go before Agent Allan arrived. Gavin became agitated and pushed Benjamin away. During the scuffle, I picked up the tracker and placed it in my pocket."

Passing the bloodstained tracker to Spencer, he said, "I don't think Benjamin knew that the tracker had live audio capabilities. Not sure how big the memory is, but you should be able to retrieve some audio conversations."

"Benjamin is working with you?"

As Detective Walker began to read Agent Allan his rights, he yelled out, "Fuck you, Walker! You're dead!"

CHAPTER

42

The back porch was Helen's favourite spot in the morning to enjoy some quiet time with her best friend Daisy.

Moving slightly on the rickety old chair, Helen said, "Good morning, sweetie. Come and enjoy the morning sun with your mummy."

Daisy was always eager to please her human mum, but today she was distracted. Running away from Helen, she began growling.

"What is it girl? Come, Daisy!"

Helen knew something was wrong when she heard a yelp followed by a thud.

Also, in his backyard and hearing breaking glass, Helen's neighbour Len looked over at her. He put a finger to his mouth and waved at her to go inside.

Retrieving a phone from his pocket, he dialled 000, requesting the police attend a possible break-in.

Hiding in a backroom wardrobe, Helen closed her eyes and pretended she was sitting on the beach watching Daisy play in the sand. Her mobile vibrated, as a message popped up: *Police on the way! Len.*

Listening to the police radio, Constable Black checked the logs as she knocked on the office wall where Walker and Spencer were working.

"Break-in, Yarras residence. Address sounded familiar. Helen Poulos, reported finding the body of Dr Marinov in the park. Local police are en route."

The patrol car arrived at the address to see Helen leaving the house with a young Caucasian man.

Approaching the pair, one of the constables asked, "Constable Ash, everything ok here?"

"False alarm, officer."

Helen looked shaken, and had suffered a bruise on her forehead.

Looking at Helen, the constable asked, "You ok, Mrs Poulos?"

With his taser drawn, her partner stared at Helen's hands shaking and said, "Sir, step away. Sir, please step away."

Pushing Helen towards the officers, the young man started running towards his car. The male constable took chase and tackled him to the ground.

As the man struggled, the constable yelled, "Stay down!"

Removing handcuffs from his belt, he secured the man on the ground, still calling out for him to stop struggling, before confirming to the radio room that an offender had been apprehended.

Seeing the ordeal was over, Helen's neighbour Len left his house and approached her. As the male officer placed the man in the back of the patrol car, his partner spoke to her. "You have a bruise on your forehead. Are you hurt anywhere else?"

"No, I'm ok. Just happy it's over."

Comforting her, Len said, "I called the police when I heard breaking glass."

"Daisy!"

"With a heavy heart, Len said, "I'm sorry, Helen. She's gone."

"Will you stay with her, sir?" the constable asked.

"Yes, of course."

Returning to the police car, the constable contacted the radio room, advising they had the offender in custody and were now returning to the police station.

Len accompanied Helen inside her house. "Would you like me to make you a cuppa? I know that I need one."

"Yes, thank you, Len."

"I will take care of Daisy. You stay inside."

Waiting for Len to leave the house, Helen looked at her watch. Seeing that his on-air programme would now be finished, she phoned Michael.

Michael answered the phone. "Helen. Nice to hear from you."

There was silence at the other end of the phone.

"Helen, is everything ok?"

"A man broke into my house today, Michael. He killed my dog Daisy."

"This is a quiet town, too much of a coincidence after everything that has happened. I am going to go to the police and tell them everything. Are you ok?"

"Yes, my neighbour called the police and they have taken him away."

"Helen, we are both involved in this. I will meet you at the police station. Tell me what time you will be there."

"Ok, I'm on my way!"

CHAPTER

43

Michael remained in his car once he'd arrived at the police carpark and waited for Helen to arrive.

They walked into the police station together. The same constable who had been at Helen's place earlier asked, "Everything ok, Mrs Poulos?"

"Yes. Um, my name is Michael Browne, a friend of Mrs Poulos. We would like to speak with the detectives working on the bunker fire case."

"They are not working at this police station; may I ask what it is regarding?"

"We only want to speak with the detectives working on the bunker case."

"Let me see if I can get the detectives on the phone."

Walking away from the reception area, Constable Ash looked at the database to find the names of the detectives assigned to the bunker fire case.

The constable phoned the Port Macquarie Police Station. "Constable Ash from Yarras. I need to speak with the detectives working on the bunker fire case."

"Yes, just a moment and I will get a detective."

Knocking on the office door, Constable Black said, "I have Constable Ash from Yarras Police Station. She wants to speak with the detectives working on the bunker fire case. This is the constable that arrested the offender who broke into the home of Helen Poulos earlier today."

"Detective Walker, how can I assist you, Constable?"

"Mrs Poulos and her friend Michael Browne are here at the station and would like to speak with you."

"Can you set up a room where we can talk? Also put the phone on speaker, thank you."

Taking Helen and Michael into an empty office, the constable put the phone on speaker and said, "Mrs Poulos and Michael are with me."

"Detective Walker speaking. How can I assist you?"

Looking at Michael, Helen said, "I found Dr Marinov burnt and injured in the park earlier this week."

"Mrs Poulos, in your statement you stated that Dr Marinov was already deceased when you discovered his body."

"Detective, my name is Michael, Michael Browne from ABC radio. Dr Marinov was a dear friend of mine. Helen did find him alive but, at his request, and, I believe, to protect her, told her to say that he was already dead when she discovered him.

"I have a recorded voice message from Dr Marinov that I would like to play, which I believe will give you a greater understanding as to why Helen did what she did."

"Yes, please play the recording."

On the completion of the recording, Detective Walker said, "That was a lot to ask of you, Helen."

"Yes, but I needed to honour his wishes and play the recording to Michael at the radio station. He also gave me a PO box key and told me not to tell anyone about the key, other than Michael."

"Do you still have the key?"

"Yes. When Agent Allan visited my house, he asked if I took anything from Dr Marinov, and I lied and said no."

"Can you please give Constable Ash the key so the contents can be taken back to the station?"

"Our little town is very quiet. I can't remember the last time a crime was committed here. Today when this man broke into my house, he hit me in the face and asked me if I took a key from Dr Marinov. He then said Agent Allan would sort me out. He killed my dog Daisy. Thinking that I would be next, I knew that I had to tell you everything."

"Thank you very much for coming forward with the key, Helen. Constable Ash will take the key from you and will retrieve the contents from the box and forward them to me. Is there anything else we can help you with before we let you go?"

Looking at each other, Helen and Michael both said, "No, thank you for your help."

CHAPTER

44

It was just before noon when Detectives Walker and Spencer received a box from Yarass Police Station.

Standing side by side, the detectives opened the box to reveal a cassette player, cassettes and two journals, both named *Dr Alex Marinov.*

Entering an office at the rear of the station, Walker asked, "Read or listen?"

Spencer had already decided. He plugged the player into a power socket. "Let's listen."

He placed cassette 1 into the device. The recording was a bit scratchy but still audible. They both looked at each other in growing horror as they listened.

"Monday, 4 January 1994, outback, South Australia. Subject 1, female 20 years."

A male voice with an accent said, "Thick rope secured her arms to the chair. Wooden splinters have dug deep into her skin, causing a trickle of blood to drip onto the concrete floor. One eye is taped open and the other taped closed."

The more the detectives heard, the more they formed the opinion that the man on the tape was torturing this young woman.

Moving the journal to one side, they decided to listen to another tape, this one labelled "Secret conversation," dated 5 July 2017.

There were three male voices in the conversation: Agent Allan, Dr Marinov and a third man who identified himself as Henry.

"Can we go back to the first cassette? I could be mistaken, but I think Henry and the man on the first cassette are the same person," Spencer said.

After listening to both recordings Spencer and Walker both agreed that Henry's voice was on both tapes.

"So, Dr Marinov and Henry have worked together before, on another secret experiment!" Walker said.

Picking up his mobile, he said, "I think it's time we updated the commander on what we have just discovered."

"Commander, Walker and Spencer here; you are on speaker. We have emptied Dr Marinov's PO box. Very interesting reading and listening material inside. Dr Marinov had two journals and a number of taped sessions in his possession. This isn't the first time Dr Marinov has been involved with experiments. The first was in 1994 in outback South Australia. Dr Marinov also recorded a conversation between himself, Agent Allan and a man named Henry. The contents of the box have been handed over as evidence."

There was silence for a few seconds before the commander replied, "Good work, Detectives."

CHAPTER
45

Arriving at Port Macquarie Police Headquarters, Walker's mobile danced on the dashboard as Spencer said, "Seriously, Peter, you need to get a new ring tone. My father has that ring tone. Exactly how old are you, mate?"

"Funny man," Walker replied.

Answering his mobile, he said, "Detective Walker!"

"It's Tim Mathers from the ME's office. I just emailed you the report on our Jane Doe."

"Thanks, Tim. I'm just logging into my email now."

Opening Tim's email, Walker and Spencer read the ME report. They looked at each other with mouths open.

Constable Black entered the room just as Spencer said, "Last line, scarecrow tattoo right upper outer thigh. Our Jane Doe is Ella Murphy!"

Looking at the constable, Walker said, "Spencer noticed the tattoo when we interviewed Ella at her home. Black,

can you check to see if there was a disturbance reported at Ella Murphy's address in the last two weeks?" he
asked.

Constable Black returned to Walker and Spencer a few
minutes later.

"The only report received was of a barking dog two
doors down from Ella's place. The constables on patrol
reported all was quiet when they arrived. Checking the
nearby properties, they only saw a dog barking at a cat
having a standoff. I'll ask the local police to take a drive
by Ella Murphy's place and check to see if there was a
disturbance."

When Constable Rogers arrived at Ella Murphy's place,
he noticed the back door was ajar. When he entered the
house, he could see trinkets lying on the kitchen floor,
but there were no real signs of a struggle.

Picking up his radio, the constable called Constable
Black. "This is Constable Rogers from Belltrees Police.
We are at the residence of Ella Murphy, 54 Rudolph
Street, Belltrees. No evidence of a struggle, but we did
find a pair of latex gloves which we have bagged and will
be taken in for evidence. We have begun taking forensic
samples. A full report will be issued asap."

CHAPTER
46

Dr Raelene Attard, ME, frowned as Detective Walker and Constable Black greeted her at the possible crime scene in Arthur Street.

"Since you arrived in town, Detective, we have been spending a lot of time together! Nothing like the smell of rotting flesh. Thankfully, I haven't had lunch yet," she said as she entered the house.

After examining the body, she said, "Initial indications show that his wrists had been tied. Once I get him back to the lab, I can confirm with certainty, but it looks like a zip tie, possibly untied after the overdose. I've gone over the body and I can't find any other needle injection sites. Nothing on either arm or between the toes. But if the wrists were tied, this is not an accidental drug overdose by a first-time user. This wasn't a voluntary injection. There will be a preliminary report in your email inbox by the end of the day, but the toxicology report will take longer."

"Thanks, Dr Attard," the constable said, as she and Walker left the house.

Driving back to the station, Black took a deep breath. "Two civilians working at the bunker, Ella Murphy and Scott Kelly. Is it a coincidence that both Ella and Scott show up dead? Has Agent Allan been tidying up and eliminating possible threats that could expose him? We now know that Benjamin has been working with Allan. We know Benjamin has Gavin, but who has Susan? There are also reports that Allan threw a Molotov cocktail down the bunker manhole."

CHAPTER

47

Blindfolded and with her hands tied, Susan sobbed as she sat on the cold concrete, trying to be brave. The creaking sound of a rusty key turning and opening a lock, and metal dragged across the concrete followed by footsteps close by alerted her that someone had entered this dark and cold space.

"Hello! Who's there?" she asked.

There was no answer, only feet shuffling, followed by an echo from something being dropped on the concrete, unsettling dust particles that rose in the air and tickled her sinuses.

A soft female voice said, "Hush, don't be frightened."

Helping Susan to her feet she said, "My name is Maria. I'm going to help you sit on a chair."

Once the girl was seated, Maria removed the blindfold and untied her hands. Then she left the room. Susan became aware she was in a basement room that contained a gurney, a table, a black bag and a scary looking beared man.

"Hello, Susan! My name is Henry. I am a friend of your father and he has asked me to make you better. How does that sound? Thirsty?"

Handing her a bottle of water, he said, "Drink up, that's a good girl."

Not understanding what she was drinking, Susan soon began to feel woozy and fell asleep.

Maria rubbed her hands together, then carried Susan to the gurney and carefully laid her down before turning on the generator lights, and opening the black bag revealing the surgical instruments. Placing them neatly on the table, she continued to set up the makeshift operating room.

"I want her prepped now. We must begin within the hour," the man said as he left the room.

Maria had assisted Henry with previous surgeries but never on such a young girl.

Music playing kept her focused as she shaved Susan's head. Thick locks of black curly hair fell onto the ground.

Who or what will you become once the surgery is over? she thought to herself.

Standing back and checking that everything was in place, she left the room to advise Henry that Susan was ready.

Henry and Benjamin were having a heated argument when Maria entered the adjoining room.

"You had simple instructions: get rid of Dr Marinov. He was a liability when he refused to work with us. Instead, you let him experiment on himself. Dr Marinov kept a journal. Have you been able to locate it? God knows what he wrote in the journal, more importantly who he told."

Before Benjamin could reply, Henry said, "Now get out. I have work to do."

He regarded himself as the father of robotic surgery. The fact that the recipients were unaware of what he was doing didn't disturb him at all.

Listening to Beethoven and with a skull saw in hand, he said, "Let's begin!"

CHAPTER

48

Sitting quietly, Agent Allan waited for his superiors to enter the interview room.

Turning on the recorder, Special Agent Evans said, "Time is 2:40pm. My name is Special Agent Evans. Also present is Special Agent Williams and the accused, Agent Brian Allan. Agent Allan, you have been arrested on suspicion of arson, kidnapping, and suspicion for the murders of Ella Murphy and Scott Kelly. We found the boat Opportunities. We know you have been working with Benjamin."

"No comment."

"Where are Susan and Gavin?"

"No comment."

Allan made no eye contact with either agent as he said, "I don't know what you are talking about. Susan is with her mother."

"That horrible day when you ran over your daughter. Every father's nightmare. We are filling in the gaps, Agent Allan. Managing the bunker would allow you to take your daughter along, and maybe the doctor could fix her. You and Henry must have been disappointed with Dr Marinov when he said he wouldn't experiment on Susan."

Allan looked at Agent Evans, as if by mentioning Henry, he had touched a nerve. "You don't know anything. I have nothing further to say."

The detectives were outside the interview room, listening.

Searching his contacts on his mobile, Walker looked at Spencer as he said, "Constable Black, can you check the database and see if you can find anything on Agent Allan's wife and daughter? Not sure if his wife now goes by her maiden name. His daughter is 16."

"Where are you going with this?" Spencer asked.

"Let's see if Allan's ex-wife reported her daughter missing. Why else would he go out of his way and organise Norman Fitzgerald to, firstly, go to the bunker and ask deliberate questions about 'the girl' and 'did she get out?' and then try and take her out of the hospital? He wanted to keep her safe."

"Pamela Allan did lodge a missing person's report for her daughter three months ago, but then withdrew, stating that Susan was staying with her father," Black reported.

CHAPTER

49

"Good morning, listeners. I'm Michael Browne, coming to you live from ABC North Coast Radio 771. Welcome to the programme. I have a busy show this morning. Finally, the heatwave is over. I don't know about you, but I am certainly feeling a chill in the air. My doona is on the bed.

"Today, I want to start off with the story that broke the news late last year, dubbed 'The Mystery Machine.'

"It has been several months since rogue ASIO agent Brian Allan was arrested and charged with arson, kidnapping and murder. He is being held without bail pending his trial. Allan was the agent managing the 'secret bunker experiments.'

"Our news reporter Neville King is reporting live from Downing Street.

"Good morning, Neville. Big day today for law enforcement agencies."

"Good morning, Michael. Absolutely. I am standing on the steps of the Downing Centre District Court where the trial of former ASIO agent Brian Allan will commence in about 30 minutes. Allan was arrested and charged with arson, and the kidnapping and murder of Ella Murphy and Scott Kelly, both employees at the Bell-trees bunker. The trial is expected to take between three to five days. You may recall Allan has never revealed the whereabouts of his daughter Susan, Michael."

"Thank you, Neville.

"There you have it, listeners. Every reporter from radio, television and newspaper will be covering this historic event.

"My telephone number is 131771. The lines are now open, give me a call."

Before Michael could take any calls, Troy, his assistant, held up a sign: *Go to an ad break!*

He held up another sign that read, *you need to check your email inbox!*

An email with the subject line titled "Susan" took a while to open.

Clicking on the attachment, Michael sat back in his chair, completely stunned.

A hologram image of Susan showed that modifications had been made to her appearance. He saw her lips move and heard the words that she said.

"The Bunker Fiend begins now!"

THE END